Alright, la

By

John Peters

Copyright © 2019 John Peters

All rights reserved, including the right to reproduce this book, or portions thereof in any form. No part of this text may be reproduced, transmitted, downloaded, decompiled, reverse engineered, or stored, in any form or introduced into any information storage and retrieval system, in any form or by any means, whether electronic or mechanical without the express written permission of the author.

All characters, events and certain places aforementioned in the novel are fictitious and any similarity to such described is purely coincidental.

ISBN: 978-0-244-80981-2

Acknowledgement

Male silhouette figures shown in the front cover design were created by www.freepik.com

To my family.

Chapter One

Who's gettin' ales in shouted a voice in the packed Weavers Arms.

It was Alan standing by the entrance door. Being a typical Friday night, the pub was rammed with people getting pissed before setting off to the local nightclub - the Oasis.

Paul, Johnny shouted above the noise of the packed bar.

You're fuckin' jokin', replied Rob, he's tighter than a crab's arse and that's water tight !

Paul, although a mate, was tight-fisted and was reputed to be able to peel an orange in his fuckin' pocket !

I'll get them, Johnny said, pint then lads?

Yeah, came the unanimous reply.

We're sat over there, indicated Johnny to Alan as he went to the bar pushing through the dense throng congregated in the bar area. He reached the bar and issued his order to an elderly barman looking agitated who was wearing a stained shirt with a Woodbine cigarette adhered to his bottom lip. He's on the pull tonight, thought Johnny.

Johnny brought the 'Walkers Warrington' ales over on a battered tin tray and joined in the banter and piss taking with the other lads. They talked of music, football and girls, what else? Who's shagged this one and who's gonna shag that one!

The pub was pretty run down but it was central and the alcohol cheap. The beer was drunk and this time Alan bought the round.

Oasis then lads? said Alan.

Too fucking right. It had to be. It was the only decent club in town.

Besides Johnny, there was Alan his best mate, Paul, Phil and Rob. There were others around who would meet up later but these five lads were close mates and had known each a number of years. About ten or twelve would regularly meet up and go out. They dressed to impress in bespoke suits, smart shirts and ties. The Oasis had a dress code; fuck knows why! Some had girl-friends but Friday was always lads' night !

At about nine o'clock, the lads amongst others left the pub and headed for the club, a little way across the town, passing the Boots' chemist store on the corner and the Odeon cinema, known as the flea-pit !

They walked down the cobbled streets that were typical in the Lancashire mining and cotton town of Cockshaw.

The entrance to the club was jammed as people pushed their way to enter. Familiar faces could be seen and winks, nods and smiles were made to the many girls who were hoping to get a pull from one of the lads. Inside they made their way to the bar, passing the many girls dying to be noticed, and stood waiting to order the pints of beer masquerading as alcohol.

The club had been a dance hall years ago with a balcony overlooking the large dance floor. It had two bars and mirrored pillars which reflected those dancing on the sprung wooden floor.

Mine's a Brown ale and bitter, said Paul cheekily.
Get your fuckin' own someone shouted.
I'm fuckin' skint ! replied Paul defensively.
You're always skint, Johnny retorted as he distributed the pint glasses and bottles of beer to the other lads.
Paul fucked off in search of a mug to stand him a beer.
He's such a fuckin' tight arse ! stressed Rob.
Leave it Rob, said Alan in Paul's defence.
Alan and Paul had known each other since childhood. Rob looked at Alan and shook his head.

Now where's these girls? stated Johnny, holding a pint glass and eagerly looking around the dance floor throbbing to the hits of the late nineteen sixties !

Spotting a pretty blonde, he walked towards the edge of the dance floor, catching her eye as she danced to the beat of the music. She was almost as tall as him with shoulder length hair and a slim figure, dressed in a tight mini-dress which displayed her shapely legs and thighs. He stood there transfixed until the music had stopped.

My name's John but you can call me Johnny he said loudly and cockily to the blonde as she walked off the dance floor.

I know who you are, she replied walking towards him with another girl.

I'm gettin' a reputation he thought as he finished his drink and left the glass on an adjacent table.

What's your name, love? he asked.

Barbara.

Well Barbara, d'you fancy a drink?

I'll get off, said her dancing companion, and join the others.

No, protested Johnny, we could have a threesome, know what I mean?

Fuck off, said the other girl tartly as she stormed off.

You've upset her, said the blonde looking annoyed, I'd better go and see to her.

She'll be alright, said Johnny reassuringly, one of me mates is bound to pull such a charmin' girl like her.

You sure?

Scouse honour, he replied knowingly.

Ok, said Barbara holding Johnny's arm as they strolled around the club.

They soon found Alan who was surrounded by a large group of people. He regularly dealt cannabis and pills and had many customers.

Watch out for the bouncers ! warned Johnny.

That's sorted, said Alan cockily.

Who's the blonde? he inquired to Johnny as he looked her up and down.

My name's Barbara, she replied coyly.

Watch him, love, Alan added, he's a randy bastard !

Johnny just grinned at that remark.

More people joined the gathering as the drugs were sold and taken away discreetly.

Come on, love, Johnny said to Barbara, I promised you a drink.

They made their way to the downstairs bar and waited. Soon Johnny was served by a middle-aged barmaid who would sooner be elsewhere!

Drinks in hand, they found a quiet corner table in the club and began to talk.

What's all this about a randy bastard?

You Liverpool lads need to be watched !

It's the drugs, said Johnny defensively, his brain is addled.

I know all about you Johnny, she stated.

All bad, I hope !

Barbara laughed and took a drink of the glass of white wine. You're in there lad said Johnny to himself. They talked some more for the rest of the night, punctuated with a couple of dances and a few more drinks until the club was about to close.

Where do you live? he asked.

Bullstock, she replied, but I've got a lift.

Can I see you again? he asked confidently.

Sure. Here's my number which she scrawled on a piece of paper and gave it to him.

Johnny looked at the number and smirked.

They kissed and he bid farewell.

I told you he was a randy bastard, said Alan, as he walked past them and out of the club with a girl on each arm.

It was one o'clock on Saturday morning and outside the Oasis there was still a gathering; the street lights shining on the faces of those reluctant to go on their way.

Let's play football, suggested Phil.

Don't be fuckin' soft, said Rob, we've got no fuckin' ball !

Bollocks, replied Phil as he walked towards a zebra crossing, climbed one of the posts and retrieved the yellow globe on top.

It's made of hard plastic and bounces like fuck, he announced triumphantly.

Phil was mainly the butt of the lads' jokes but would do anything to be noticed. He was tall with a shock of dark hair, gangly in appearance and a bit of a dark horse. He never spoke of his home or personal life only that he worked in a warehouse. Being dyslexic, he thought the job he got was in a whorehouse !

Phil threw the globe into the crowd who chased after it eagerly and smacked it against the adjacent shop frontages.

Fuck this, said Rob inspecting his smart Italian shoes.

Johnny's shoes were well scuffed as he powered in a few shots. Funny, no-one wanted to keep goal. After a while a police car siren signalled the end of the game and everyone walked off shouting good-natured abusive remarks to each other.

Johnny lived in the west of town and was joined by Alan and Phil as he walked homewards in the cold early morning. Along the way the night's events were discussed.

I made a few bob, boasted Alan, recapping on his drug dealing exploits.

Those bouncers leave me alone 'cause I cut them in.

And I kopped off with two sisters, he bragged.

Wondered where you were, stated Phil.

Up the alley behind the Oasis, both hands busy, added Alan.

Just your hands, winked Phil.

Goodnight all round, said Johnny but thinking dozy bastard will get fucked by drugs one day.

As they walked on, they saw a redundant lamp-post laying at the side of the road.

Lazy fuckin' council can't even take it away, remarked Johnny.

Come on, said Alan, I've got an idea. We'll lay it across the road.

Fuck off, shouted Johnny, you fuckin' maniac.

No, protested Alan, it'll be a laugh.

The three of them picked up the lamp-post and laid it across the road causing an obstruction.

Careless council shit-heads, declared Johnny which brought a laugh from the other two. The three of them proceeded to walk on towards their destinations. It was turned two in the morning and there wouldn't be any traffic at that time of night.

CRASH! BANG!

What the fuck was that? Well it was obvious. Some stupid nob-head driving well over the speed limit, had run into the lamp-post. None of them decided to go back and see the carnage and continued onwards.

Chapter Two

Early afternoon, Johnny arose from his bed, worse for wear after the previous night's excesses. Suddenly he remembered and frantically searched his discarded clothes for Barbara's number. He found it, barely legible on a piece of screwed up paper. A sense of relief jolted him into sobriety.

After a shower, he dressed quickly, slipping on a pair of faded Levi jeans and a pale blue sweater. He combed his damp hair. On his way out of the house, he grabbed a chicken leg, recently cooked, from the kitchen table.

This isn't a hotel, shouted his mother.

It was about one-thirty in the afternoon as Johnny waited impatiently for a bus in the warm spring sunshine. He quickly scoffed the chicken leg and discarded the bone into the road. The bus would be going into town. Where else?

As he waited for the bus, he reflected on the previous night. His first thought was of the lamp-post and the stupid cunt who had driven into it. Then he remembered Barbara.

It wasn't long before the bus came. Johnny boarded, paid his fare and sat down on the lower deck. He looked out the window as the bus passed the neat red-brick terraced houses which lined both

sides of the long road into town. He thought about Barbara the girl he had met the night before.

The bus arrived at its destination and Johnny alighted.

Alright lad ! he shouted to a familiar face.

Sound came the reply. It was Rob who had spent the night with his girl-friend, Jane. Rob was another scouser who didn't live in the town but spent the week-end with Jane at her house then would go back to Liverpool.

Weavers, they both agreed and made their way to the pub.

Inside the usual suspects were present, laughing, joking and supping beer. A loud cheer greeted the arrival of Johnny and Rob. The beer was bought and they both joined the others. The conversation turned to the previous nights events and plans for that evening. It was usual for them to go to Blackpool to the Mecca ballroom by coach. Tickets had been bought and about forty would be on the coach leaving Market Square.

Did you hear about the crash? someone said.

What fuckin' crash? Johnny asked winking at Alan.

A fuckin' car drove into a lamp-post at speed. No injuries but the car's a fuckin' write-off.

What's unusual about that? Alan inquired, tongue in cheek.

The post was laid in the fuckin' road.

Lazy council twats, Johnny exclaimed.

Right nob-heads someone added which started ripples of laughter.

More beer was bought and drank as the jokes and banter descended into obscenities.

Closing time came and the gang of lads cascaded into the street.

See you tonight was the parting comment as several drifted away.

Johnny, Rob and Alan were left talking outside the Weavers Arms with its dilapidated red and white facade crying out for some tender loving care or a wrecking ball !

She was a bit of alright that blonde, said Alan, seein' her again?

Christ ! shouted Johnny, I've forgot to ring her.

He's in love, joked Rob.

Smitten, added Alan.

Fuck off you two, said Johnny grinning.

They soon found a phone booth and the three of them piled in.

Johnny searched his pockets and found the piece of paper with Barbara's number written on it. He dialled the number, put a coin in the slot and waited.

Hello came a reply.

Can I speak to Barbara? said Johnny confidently.

Who's that?

It's John, er Johnny.

Wait a minute was the reply.

Hi Johnny.

Hi Barbara.

So you rang then? added Barbara.

Well, yes.

The other two started to make noises down the mouth-piece of the phone.

Who's with you? she demanded

Just two little pricks called Alan and Rob.

Barbara laughed.

Listen, said Johnny, fancy goin' out tomorrow night?

Love to, replied Barbara.

Right. I'll meet you outside the railway station at eight.

OK, she said.

'Bye, love, said Johnny as he replaced the receiver banging and thumping the coin box without success.

Come on you two nob-heads ! said Johnny as the three of them walked through the town looking in the various mens' clothes shops, looking at the various mini-skirted girls and making mental notes of both.

Chapter Three

The Market Square was packed that Saturday evening with people waiting to board the various coaches that would transport them out of the town. All the lads were suited and booted in their bespoke clobber, Ben Sherman shirts and smart shoes.

The coach for Blackpool duly arrived and the excited throng jostled to be first aboard and bag the rear seats.

Nods and pleasantries were exchanged by friends and acquaintances which wouldn't be repeated by the end of the evening.

Everyone here? asked Alan.

Looks like it, replied Johnny glancing around the coach.

Those lads courting had brought their girl-friends along. The single lads were always on the look-out for one-night stands - even the girls spoken for weren't safe.

Where's Rob? someone asked.

He's not here, Alan stated, Jane put her foot down.

Whoa! came the united response.

She's a miserable cow, piped up Phil.

Thought you were asleep or dead, laughed Jamie another one of the crowd.

Fuck off, sulked Phil.

Listen Phil, said Johnny winking at Alan, I reckon you're a snerch !

What's that? asked Alan smiling.

Yeah, said Phil, what's a fuckin' snerch?

Well, replied Johnny, the word snerch can be a noun or verb.

What d'you mean? a puzzled Phil asked.

Right, Phil, you are a snerch and your action is to snerch.

Explain your fuckin' self, said Phil impatiently.

Yeah, Johnny explain, said half the passengers.

Well, to snerch, the verb is to smell ladies' bicycle seats for sexual pleasure.

Fuckin' gross. Disgustin' groaned a few passengers, mostly girls, while the others laughed.

You've been rumbled Phil, said Jamie, I'd keep away from the convent school bike sheds in future !

He can fuckin' keep away from us said a couple of girls indignantly still retching at the thought.

Fuck off, said Phil, you're all a bunch of cunts!

Now, now Phil !

Didn't the Hollies sing about snerchin? said Jamie as an afterthought.

No, you dozy cunt, corrected Johnny, that was 'Searchin' !

The coach slowly pulled out of the cobbled square and on its way to Blackpool, passing through the northern suburbs and onto the motorway.

Where's the piss bucket? someone asked.

Haven't got one came an anonymous reply.

It would take an hour to Blackpool, so anyone desperate for a slash would have to hold on or piss themselves. The coach made its way through Preston over the Ribble viaduct and onto the coast road. This was an 'A' road that passed through Fylde, a favourite residential area of the well-heeled.

We're halfway there thought Johnny.

I'm dyin' for a piss, said Alan, I'm gonna ask the driver to stop.

Can't you wait? said Johnny.

I need to go to too, added Jamie.

And me.

And me.

And me.

Almost all the lads indicated that they wanted to slash.

Driver, said Johnny, grinning, can we stop for these fuckers?

The driver tut, tutted as he pulled over in a lay-by and the stampede to get off the coach started.

Several lads ran away from the coach to urinate in a grassed area while others including Johnny, who went to be sociable, pissed against the side of the coach in full view of the girls looking through the windows.

After finishing, they shook their cocks at the girls much to their delight.

With everyone seated, the coach proceeded on towards Blackpool.

It wasn't long before the coach pulled into the huge car park behind Bloomfield Road, the home ground of Blackpool Football Club, on Central Drive.

I'll be leaving dead on twelve midnight, said the driver as the excited party disembarked, so don't be late otherwise you'll be left behind.

Fully understood misery guts, said Alan to the driver with a wry smile upon his face.

The Mecca ballroom was just around the corner but first the lads went in search of a beer before going into the dance - hall. They walked passed it with loads of people especially girls queuing up to go in.

There's plenty of pussy here tonight someone remarked.

And I've got plenty of cream that they'll enjoy, laughed Jamie pulling on his crotch.

Jamie wasn't one of the regular crowd but hung around with the lads and lived east of the town with his younger brother and mother. His father having passed away when he was a teen. He worked as a plasterer to support his mum and sibling but always dressed smart.

He fancied himself as a ladies man and would spend hours preening himself.

The Golden Mile was just ten minutes walk away with countless pubs and bars along its intoxicating front. The summer season hadn't begun but the front was packed with holiday-makers and trippers.

The sky was almost dark and the grey surf lapped against the deserted beach. A few sea-gulls flew overhead screeching in the cold breeze that blew in from the Irish Sea. The neon signs and lights of the pubs and bars shone brightly beckoning the punters.

The lads made their way into one such bar and drinks were ordered and downed in rapid succession. Paul strangely put his hand in his pocket and bought a round to much cheering. More drinks were ordered but drank less enthusiastically.

What's the time someone asked.

Half - eight came a reply.

Come on, Johnny said, otherwise the best birds will be pulled.

The lads drank up and made their way to the Mecca. There was no queue and they walked straight in while being scrutinised by the door-men. It was customary to sign in at the Mecca and the lads duly obliged after paying the entrance fee. A few pseudonyms were scribed including a Richard Head, a Wayne King and a Mike Hunt ! There were five of them as they walked up the staircase into the Highland Room which had a dance-floor surrounded by tables and a DJ sat on a raised platform playing the latest R&B hits. The music stopped and the DJ Tony, recognizing Johnny and his entourage, said

This is for the Cockshaw lads as he took out a disc and put it on the turn-table. Johnny acknowledged Tony with the usual thumbs-up ! 'Dancing Master ' by Palmer Jones blasted from the sound system; this was their signature tune and had been for some time. It was also played regularly at the Oasis Club. Most of the coach party was there and various girls came up to the boys. The cock waving incident had made quite an impression.

Johnny and Alan made their way to the long bar which ran the full length of the Highland Room leaving the other three to mingle and chat with the girls from the coach. The bar staff, male and female were young and smart, who served them efficiently.

A beer and whiskey was carried by each as they made their way to a vacant table where they sat and watched various girls performing on the dance floor to the pulsating sounds coming from Tony's deck.

You haven't brought any gear? asked Johnny.

Fuck sake no, replied Alan, these bouncers are too keen as he lit a straight cigarette.

So you've got a date Johnny, added Alan taking a long draw on the cigarette.

This could be serious?

No, Johnny replied, she's just another notch on the belt.

Look, I'm twenty, he added, too young to get tied down.

Watch this space, Alan joked and the two clinked glasses.

There you are a voice said I've been lookin' for you's.

It was soft-lad Phil.

What is it, nob - head? answered Johnny disinterested.

Listen, added Phil, lets go moose huntin'. We each pull an ugly girl and compare.

We could have saved time if you had brought your sister, said Alan grinning.

FUCK YOU BOTH, shouted Phil loudly which attracted the attention of a couple of bouncers dressed in dinner jackets and black bow ties.

Everything alright? said one of them glaring at the trio.

Sound, said Johnny apologetically, just a family matter.

Phil fucked off and Johnny and Alan laughed.

You wicked bastard, said Johnny, he's a mate.

A soft one at that, added Alan, and he fuckin' snerches.
They both laughed again and finished their Scotch whisky.

From the corner of his eye, Johnny sensed he was being watched by some fucking no-mark usually wanting to start a fight.

That fat bastard over there is pipin' me, said Johnny to Alan.

I've seen him before his name his Dougie, a loner and so-called hard cunt from Glasgow, replied Alan, he's a regular here.

Figures, replied Johnny. It is the Highland Room and I suppose he must have a tartan cock !

Both laughed.

Johnny looked over to where the fat cunt was standing and glaring at him.

Hey, nob-head, Johnny shouted, do you want me photograph or autograph?

The fat Jock walked over. He was as tall as Johnny but a lot heavier with curly light brown hair.

Johnny and Alan rose from their seats.

Yer a fuckin' prick, said fat Jock, yer a fuckin' cunt, yer flash fucker !

Johnny felt his heart race and the adrenalin rushing around his body.

The feelin's mutual, laughed Johnny as he turned towards Alan smiling and then looked back at the fat bastard and said

Hey, nob-head, wanna run my fan club?

Fat Jock wasn't happy. His rotund face turned crimson and his fists were now clenched. It's now or never thought Johnny.

BANG!

, Johnny head - butted fat Jock and he reeled th blood exploding from his nose.

in again smashing his fists against his fat face ered. More blood was now cascading down fat ugly countenance as he reeled backwards and onto the floor where Johnny continued pummelling his face without reply from the tartan turd.

The bouncers soon intervened, pulling both of them apart. Fat Jock, with blood over his face, was taken away and Johnny was being escorted off the premises by two bouncers.

Get off me, you pricks ! protested Johnny to the meat heads.

Oi, mate, said Alan to one of the meat heads, he didn't start it. That mad Jock was to blame. He's a fuckin' maniac you should bar him.

After explaining and arguing Johnny's case, the bouncers relented and let him stay in the club.

But anymore trouble and you're both out, one said firmly.

That was a result, said Johnny, thanks mate.

But watch out for that Jock cunt, Johnny, said Alan.

He looks a nasty bastard!

It'll be sound, added Johnny triumphantly, especially after the scouse kiss he got !

Alan grinned at that remark.

Three girls came over to the duo along with some of the boys.

You alright Johnny? was the general inquiry asked by all. He answered in the affirmative which made those around him feel better.

Come on said one girl you need a drink.

See you later, lad, said Alan as he joined the others chatting up several girls.

I'll have a Brandy and Babycham, said the girl walking Johnny to the long bar.

You will fuck Janet, replied Johnny, it'll be a glass of beer !

Tight arse, laughed Janet snuggling closer to him and holding onto his arm.

Johnny ordered the two beers and they found a table in a quiet darkened corner of the club.

Janet was known to him as one of the regular crowd around Cockshaw and pretty liberal with her sexual favours. She was pretty and slim with black short hair and brown eyes, wearing a mini – dress which highlighted her shapely legs. He couldn't understand why he'd never fucked her !

You know I fancy you, said Janet.

That's nice, replied Johnny, but I thought you were with someone. You've always got lads sniffin' around.

There's no-one special, she added.

She smiled and winked at him which made Johnny feel unguarded as he thought of tomorrow's date with Barbara. No doubt he fancied Janet but he had never two-timed any girl in his life. Probably, because he wasn't long enough with them ! This is fucking awkward he said to himself. He looked at Janet, smiled and kissed her lightly on the lips. Janet pulled Johnny towards herself and kissed him deep. Her tongue searching the cavity of his mouth and finding his tongue. Another deep kiss followed and Johnny could feel the passion stirring inside him. What the fuck Johnny thought. I've not been on a date yet with Barbara. It might not work out and here's a bird in my hand beggin' to be shagged !

For a couple of hours or so, they chatted, danced, drank and kissed.

Let's go outside, love, suggested Johnny, its eleven fifteen plenty of time before the coach leaves.

But I'm stayin' in Blackpool, replied Janet, me and a couple of girls have got a room for the week-end. It was booked in the week.

Well, I'll walk you to it, suggested Johnny.

Ok, replied Janet, let me tell the others.

Johnny waited and several mates came over, with girls at their sides.

You pulled? asked Phil himself with a girl on his arm.

Looks like it, Johnny replied with a bemused look on his face.

Meet my girl, chipped in Phil proudly.

Standing beside him was the most ugliest female Johnny had seen. Phil had exceeded himself.

Hello, love, said Johnny, you local?

No, came the reply, from Leeds.

You haven't cycled here? he further asked.

No, she fuckin' hasn't, interjected Phil indignantly.

Lovely city that Leeds, added Johnny, famous for beautiful women and great rugby league players.

The girl smiled.

Looking closely into her face, Johnny said,

What position do you play, love?

Everyone around fell about laughing.

FUCK OFF, shouted Phil and dragged the moose away.

See you on the coach various people said to Johnny as they drifted away; some with companions and others not as Janet rejoined Johnny.

All sorted, she said, got me flat key.

Well then let's go, said Johnny as they walked to the exit hand in hand and down the staircase earlier climbed.

Outside it was cold and dark and he took off his jacket and wrapped it around Janet.

Your such a gent, Johnny, she said gratefully.

All part of the service, love, he replied gripping her hand tighter and thinking definitely a shag on here.

Where to? he asked as they walked along the deserted Blackpool streets. Barely audible were the sounds from the Golden Mile – music from the bars and the laughing and shouting of the numerous revellers – which greeted their progress to Janet's flat.

It's not far just down here, she indicated.

Good, said Johnny, I need warmin' up and a piss as he pulled her into an alley which ran behind the rows of guest houses.

Johnny undid his zip, pulled out his cock and slashed against the brick wall. The steam from his piss rose into the damp night air. Janet giggled.

That's twice I've seen that.

Twice ! Johnny said.

Yeah, she explained, now and outside the coach.

Johnny remembered and laughed.

I'm spoilin' you, Janet, he said.

He moved closer to Janet and kissed her long and hard with one hand fondling her breasts and the other between her legs as his cock hardened.

Oi, protested Janet, it's my time of month you can't !

Sorry, apologized Johnny, but you can't blame me for tryin'.

I do like you Johnny, she said, but not now.

Ok, he replied, I'll just have to be patient.

You've got a reputation and I'm not goin' to be another notch on your belt not yet, she added.

Johnny laughed, saying

And you haven't got a reputation?

Janet smiled.

Come on lets go, she suggested.

Suddenly, a flash- light shone up the alley and the figure of a policeman was clearly visible to both.

Hello, officer, said Johnny, you're wearin' a bigger helmet than she's seen tonight.

A comedian, eh? replied the copper sternly.

On yer way, you two, he added.

Johnny quickly fastened his trouser zip and they both followed PC Plod out of the dark alley and into the illuminated street.

It's down here, Janet indicated walking Johnny to a large guest house with a neon VACANCY sign flashing brightly.

The Blackpool Hilton, remarked Johnny causing Janet to giggle.

They briefly kissed and Janet turned the key to the front door.

I'll see you again Jan, when the red shirt's left the field, said Johnny taking his jacket from her shoulders and putting it back on himself.

Sure, she smiled, I'll see you in the Oasis some time.

Waving, she closed the door behind her.

Johnny smiled to himself. Two birds keen on me and both lookers, even though one's a slag.....it must be Christmas.

He looked at his chronograph watch. It was eleven fifty. The coach would leave in ten minutes. Where the fuck am I? he panicked.

And where's the coach parked?

Walking bristly he retraced his steps from the Mecca ballroom. I'm sure we came down here he said to himself reassuringly.

He found his way to Central Drive. Not far to the coach now. Walking hurriedly past a few shop fronts, he could see the Mecca ballroom in the distance and a few late revellers' drunkenly shouting at each other. The coach and the others will be 'round the corner.

Hey yoo Jimmy....I want yoo !

Johnny recognized the voice. It was the fat Scots twat that he had battered earlier. The cunt must have waited outside the Mecca and followed me with Jan he thought.

I'm talkin' to yoo, yoo fuckin' prick ! came another directive.

Without looking around, Johnny quickened his step. He had more important matters to do than exchanging pleasantries with some deranged Glaswegian maniac. He noticed heavy footsteps behind him. This cunt was getting closer. Then he heard FLICK the sound of a switch-blade being engaged for business. Johnny's heart raced. The walk became a jog and then a sprint. Fat Jock also began running but not as fast as Johnny. The Mecca was reached as he pushed past some drunks and ran around the corner to the car park. In the distance, he noticed his coach driving out. He ran faster and caught up with it. The fat Jock was still chasing him but some distance behind. Johnny banged frantically on the door but the coach was still mobile. Faces peered out of the windows and suddenly, the coach stopped and the door flew open.

GET IN, shouted Alan.

Johnny scrambled in, sweat trickling down his face; his heart ready to explode !

Fat Jock, his face still bloody and bruised from the battering, stood gasping for breath and watched as the coach drove out of the car park and headed back to Cockshaw. He waved the blade at the coach in a last futile attempt at intimidation.

Johnny stood at the half opened door, breathing deeply.

FUCK OFF YOU SCOTS CUNT, he managed to shout accompanied with the necessary V-sign.

Where have you been, inquired Alan, chasin' pussy no doubt?

The coach erupted in laughter.

And the pussy was wearing a Liverpool red shirt! Johnny gasped.

Alan and the rest of the coach laughed and smiled with some girls perplexed by the remark.

Jokin' aside I'm fuckin' knackered, declared Johnny, that was fuckin' close. The cunt only had a fuckin' flick knife.

Sit down here, indicated Jamie, we'll soon be back in Cockshaw. Johnny slumped in the coach seat, reflecting on the evening's events with Alan sat at his side.

Jamie sat opposite beside a pretty brunette. He looked and smiled at her. She smiled back expecting an amorous advance from him.

I can tell the day you were born by feelin' your tits, he said to her.

No you fuckin' can't, she protested a bit tipsy.

Yes I can, Jamie replied.

I don't fuckin' believe you.

Trust me, he said convincingly.

Well go on then, instructed the brunette intrigued and sceptical.

Jamie felt and groped her breasts for about thirty seconds.

Annoyed and pushing away his hands she said

Well then on what day was I born?

He looked at her, smiled and replied

Yesterday !

For a few seconds she thought and then realized.

Fuck off, she told him, slapped his face and rejoined her mates. Jamie laughed.

I suppose a date's out of the question? he shouted after her.

It was about one-twenty when the coach pulled into Market Square. The streets were deserted and cold as dozens of trippers piled out of the coach. All the mates chatted for a while and some desperate for a piss found shop doorways. Goodbyes were said to one another and some of the lads chased after the single girls hoping to get lucky.

Alan, Johnny and Phil made their way home, treading the same path the night before.

You've got that date, Johnny, reminded Alan.

Yeah, replied Johnny, but I'm fucked after the excitement tonight.

Where was fuckin' Paul tonight? Johnny asked.

Oh, he pulled an old girl-friend and went missin', replied Phil.

Just when it was his round of drinks, laughed Johnny.

To be fair he did buy some beers, added Phil.

Not for fuckin' us, Alan said begrudgingly.

Sorry about tonight Phil, takin' the piss and all, added Johnny, but that bird was so fuckin' ugly.

Are you seein' her next week? chipped in Alan.

No, replied Phil, she fuckin' lives in Leeds but I got a shag.

You dirty, sly bastard, said Johnny, more than me.

And me ! echoed Alan.

They walked on until each reached their homes avoiding the street with the lamp post.

Johnny opened the front door of the neat red brick terraced house and climbed the stairs to his bedroom. His mother and father were sleeping soundly in the front bedroom. Johnny undressed and dragged himself into bed. He thought of Janet. I'll be seeing her again he promised himself. But first there was the date with Barbara.

Chapter Four

Johnny awoke in the early afternoon and made his way downstairs wearing a pair of linen trousers and no top. He entered the kitchen and filled a glass of cold water from the tap.

Hangover? inquired his mother sarcastically.

She was a small blonde woman with a sharp Liverpudlian dialect. The family had moved to Cockshaw a number of years ago when Johnny's father had changed jobs. She doted on Johnny and he knew how to play upon her softness.

Johnny just smiled.

When's dinner? he asked.

Soon came the reply.

Good, he added, where's Dad?

Workin' on the car, his mother stated, in the garage.

The garage was located at the rear of the house accessed by a service road.

Did you go to mass today? asked Johnny to his mother.

Of course but you haven't been in months. Your soul must be as black as night.

You really must go, son, she added, otherwise Father Pat will be down on me like a ton of bricks!

Listen, mam, Jesus is lookin' after me just fine without me goin' to church, Johnny replied.

Johnny's father appeared at the kitchen door. He was a tall man, balding with a pencil moustache wearing overalls. He was an engineer and knew how to fix motors although not a motor mechanic.

Johnny didn't drive. Which was just as well with his lifestyle.

Dinner ready, love? he inquired.

Nearly, said his wife, go and get washed up.

The three of them sat at the table and she plated up the food.

It's a beef casserole she exclaimed as each began to devour the fare.

I suppose your out again tonight? asked Johnny's mother.

Yeah, got a date, replied her son.

Johnny's father opened a bottle of red wine and poured each a glass.

Bit posh this, Johnny said, we'll be movin' to Cockshaw Lane next.

It's your mother, replied his father, she's joined a wine club.

Nothing wrong with improvin' yourself, snapped his mother.

And when are you bringin' home these girl-friends? she added.

When the right one comes along, said Johnny.

Hell will freeze over first, laughed his mother.

Johnny knew that any girl he brought home would get the third degree. No-one is good enough for my son was her mantra. No wonder she was pleased that Johnny, a boy, was born. She couldn't have a girl to rival her husband's affections for her, daughter or not !

The meal was finished and the wine drunk. The table was cleared and the plates washed. Johnny's father returned to the garage while Johnny and his mother went into the lounge and put on the TV. They sat back to watch some old black-and-white film usual for a Sunday afternoon.

Soon Johnny nodded off....

He awoke with a jolt. The lounge clock showed six-fifty. Fuck, he said to himself as he raced upstairs to get ready for the date.

He entered his bedroom and laid out his clothes for that evening. Smart grey single - breasted suit, Como Italian leather shoes and a pink gingham- check Ben Sherman shirt. I'll look the dog's bollocks for this date he thought. He entered the bathroom where he showered and shaved, dowsing himself generously in Brut aftershave. He towelled dry his medium length dark hair and combed it. He stood admiring himself in the mirror. It was seven- thirty when he finally dressed, putting his keys and money in the trouser pockets of the suit.

I'm off now, he shouted slamming the front door.

He walked to the bottom of the road and saw a bus in the distance. Barbara will wait he assured himself if I'm late. The bus came and Johnny boarded it paying the fare into town. The evening was still light when he alighted at the train station. Johnny looked at his watch. It was seven-fifty five and no sign of Barbara. Let's keep her keen he said to himself as he walked into an adjacent pub. He ordered a small beer and sat by a window which looked on to the station front. Johnny took a sip of beer and watched as passengers and couples congregated around the station entrance. Suddenly, Johnny spotted Barbara quickly walking to the arranged rendez-vous. It was just after eight. I'll give her a few more minutes he thought drinking more beer from the glass.

She'll wait.

At five past eight, Johnny walked out of the pub and sauntered cockily across the forecourt of the station.

Spotting Barbara he said, Hi love.

You're late, she said annoyingly.

And so were you ! replied Johnny.

How did you know? she asked.

I was watchin' from the pub.

Barbara laughed. They kissed, held hands and walked into the town. Johnny noticed how attractive she looked. Her shoulder length blonde hair was flicked up; she was wearing a brown suede coat with matching shoes and carrying the necessary hand-bag containing probably lots of useless stuff that girls need!

Where are we going? she asked.

We'll have a drink and a stroll 'round town, stated Johnny, its a pleasant evening.

If that's OK? he added.

Yeah, replied Barbara staring into his pale blue eyes.

They made their way to a discreet bar off the main street. Johnny smiled as he glanced at the sign above the entrance - The Cock and Pussy !

Barbara sat in a secluded corner while Johnny went to the bar and waited his turn. The bar was small and intimate with art nouveau and abstract prints on the walls including the Vladimir Tretchikoff 'Chinese Lady' print. A few patrons were drinking, smoking and talking in hushed tones. They appeared a lot older than Johnny and Barbara.

White wine is it, love? he asked across the room.

Yes please Johnny, came the reply looking at him with a glint in her eye.

A young attractive bar-maid with a low cut top served him. Johnny couldn't keep his eyes off her ample cleavage. She smiled and winked as she gave him the drinks. One for the future he thought !

He brought over the glass of wine and a small beer to the table where Barbara sat.

Cheers he said and they both clinked glasses.

Now tell me about yourself, Johnny said, you seem to know a fair bit about me?

Not everything, Barbara replied, anyway I've lived all my life in Cockshaw. Mum and Dad own a business and work very hard at it.

I'm sure they do, Johnny interjected.

I have one younger sister she continued.

As pretty as you no doubt, complimenting her.

Barbara blushed and took a sip of wine.

Now where was I? she said.

Oh, yes I work for an electronics company in sales and I'm twenty-two.

Bloody 'ell, said Johnny surprised, you're two years older than me !

That a problem? queried Barbara.

No, replied Johnny, I like my women mature.

Watch it you cheeky bugger, she replied giving Johnny a playful dig to his ribs.

At twenty-two, you should be well settled by now, he added.

To be honest, she said, I've just broken up with some-one. We had been going out since our teens. I thought we'd get married but things didn't work out.

What about you? she added.

I've had a few girl-friends but no-one serious.

Johnny was being economical with the amount of girl-friends or rather casual relationships he'd had !

Quite the Casanova, laughed Barbara, maybe I'm the one Johnny?

Maybe you are, love, he said looking into her bright blue eyes.

Fuckin' 'ell, he thought she is keen.

Let's go for a walk, love, Johnny suggested.

They drank up and left the empty bar. It was almost dark as they walked through the town on this warm spring evening, passing the many watering-holes known to each other.

Tell me more about you? Barbara demanded.

Ok, he replied as they found a bench seat near the park and sat close to each other; their arms linked and their hands held tightly.

I've been livin' here for about ten years. The family moved from Liverpool. I went to the catholic boys' school.

I'm a convent girl... at least we've got something in common.

Devout mothers, replied Johnny laughing.

Barbara laughed as well.

I'll expect a few Hail Mary's and a candle lit when you're next at mass, he laughed.

On your bike ! she smiled.

They both laughed and kissed briefly.

What's your job? Barbara inquired.

I work for a large building firm doin' estimates and calculations. It's quite interestin' and I get to visit the sites sometimes.

A pen pusher, she stated.

Better than luggin' bricks and mortar around all day like Terry and Eric, lads I know.

True, she agreed.

They chatted more about likes and dislikes, mutual friends and family.

Johnny looked at his watch. The time had flown it was almost eleven o' clock.

Let's get you home, love, he said protectively.

Pity I could stay out all night, said Barbara reluctantly.

Me too, Johnny agreed, but it's Monday tomorrow and that means work. Fuck the bus, we'll get a cab !

They walked through the town and on their way encountered numerous faces known to each piling out of the various bars and pubs in the town centre. They reached the taxi rank which was near the railway station and waited.

I've enjoyed tonight, said Barbara excitedly.

Same here, agreed Johnny.

I'll ring you and arrange another date.

You'd better ! replied Barbara threateningly but in a humorous manner.

A cab came along and they jumped into it. Barbara gave the driver directions and the taxi sped off. During the journey, they chatted, laughed and kissed passionately under the watchful gaze of the cabbie.

Hey lad, keep your eyes on the road ! ordered Johnny.

The taxi arrived at the destination. The house was big and detached with outside lighting illuminating the large frontage.

Bye Johnny, Barbara said kissing him fully on the lips as she exited from the cab.

Bye, love he replied.

He saw her walk up the drive, wave and go into the house.

Where to now? asked the cabbie.

Johnny gave him directions and he slumped back into the long seat putting his feet right across it much to the annoyance of the cab driver.

Soon the taxi pulled up outside his house and he paid the fare.

Where's me tip? demanded the driver.

FUCK OFF ! shouted Johnny almost waking the neighbours.

The taxi drove off with the driver muttering the word cunt as Johnny opened the door to his house and disappeared inside.

Chapter Five

The days came and went until the week-end arrived. Johnny had telephoned Barbara and arranged another date. This time he would be taking her to dinner. This was something he'd never done. She must be special for Johnny to make such an effort. She was different to the usual slags he dated and fucked ! In the meantime, he had to meet up with the lads and sort out this summers holiday. Last year it was Spain where they all got pissed and were nearly arrested by those nice carabineros.

It was Friday night again and the lads were in the Weavers Arms. These consisted of the usual suspects Alan, Rob, Jamie, Paul, Phil, Johnny and a few others. The beers were got in, cigarettes passed around, jokes and stories exchanged.

Right lads, said Alan, we're here to discuss this summer's holiday.

I'm not goin' to fuckin' Spain again, protested Phil scoffing a meat and potato pie.

Not after that fuckin' bull chased me.

Well you did climb into that bull-ring half-pissed soft-shite, explained Johnny.

If I'd have been that matador, I would have stuck sword up your fuckin' arse, said Alan.

Everyone laughed including Phil.

Down to business lads, said Alan, let's stay local.

You mean spend our fortnight holiday in Cockshaw? queried Phil.

No, gob-shite, remonstrated Alan, in England!

Sound idea, agreed Johnny and the others.

Right then, what about Newquay in Cornwall. Jamie and Paul went there last year and they say it was ace for pullin' birds?

Some of us have girl-friends, said Rob.
Well bring Jane then, winked Johnny at Rob, or stay behind?
I'll see what she says, replied Rob sheepishly.
#Under my thumb, the girl who once had me down,
Under my thumb, the girl who once pushed me around#
sang Johnny.
The other lads looked at Rob and laughed.
That's sorted, said Alan, we're off to Newquay in July.
You'll be bringin' that Barbara then Johnny?
Who's this Barbara? asked Rob his recent embarrassment forgotten.
Oh, he's goin' steady is Johnny, Alan said, his shaggin' days will soon be over.
Fuck off, shouted Johnny, it's early days, lad.

All the lads finished their beers, left the Weavers and headed towards the Oasis Club. Inside it was business as usual, Alan sold his wacky baccy. Even the bouncers bought an ounce or two.

Jamie, Phil and Paul chatted up the girls, dancing with them in a huge circle on the dance floor. The girls' hand-bags pushed to the centre. Johnny sat with Rob, who lit up a legal cigarette. They talked and joked.

Time you moved to Cockshaw, said Johnny.

I can't move in with Jane, he said, there's no room. Remember she's still at home with her brothers.

Johnny nodded.

A number of girls passed by their table and smiled at the two lads who acknowledged them. Some, stopped and whispered before moving on.

It's like being in a sweet shop, said Rob, but I've gotta behave.

So have I, admitted Johnny.

So you're keen on this Barbara ?

Looks like it, Johnny replied.

D'you know Jane's bothers? said Rob, diverting the conversation.

Johnny shook his head.

Fuckin' rugby players, he added, play for the town's team. Big cunts. I'm handy but no match for them fuckers.

You'd better behave then Rob, smiled Johnny.

Come on, he added, let's get a beer.

If you can call it that? argued Rob.

Beers weren't bought . Instead they ordered large vodkas with tonic and Johnny proposed a toast -

Barbara and Jane and we hope they're worth it !

The drinks were gulped down and another round bought. Alan came over, a cannabis joint held discreetly in his hand which he passed to Rob who took a long draw and passed it back.

Good shit, man! he commented.

Fuckin' 'ell thought Johnny, he saw the film, Easy Rider last week and now he's gone all fuckin' hippy !

It should be, replied Alan, Lebanese Gold as he fucked off towards a group of girls who giggled excitedly at his appearance.

Rob lived in Huyton, near Liverpool, a huge housing and industrial estate built in the fifties to house the overspill created by the slum clearance of the inner city after the war years. He worked as a mechanical engineer for one of the many enterprises trading on the estate. Rob was the same age as most of the lads, twenty, but looked older. He made the trip to Cockshaw each Friday and returned on Sunday evening after his liaison with Jane.

Our days of womenizing maybe over, Rob said reluctantly.

Your days, replied Johnny, but if it don't work out with Babs, a busy bee like me intends to visit a few more honey pots.

Rob laughed.

Suddenly, a commotion was heard from the dance floor and a couple of bouncers appeared, grabbing hold of a lad who struggled to break free. They marched him off the floor, up some stairs and into the club's office.

Jamie and Alan came over and told them some toe-rag had rifled a girl's hand bag. Phil had seen it happen, grabbed the cunt and held him until the bouncers came.

Fuckin' hell they all thought, he's a hero.

The girl should be very grateful to Phil, said Rob.

She's a bit plain though, replied Jamie.

Listen, added Johnny, ugly, pretty or disabled us Phil will shag anything.

Everyone laughed.

Phil and Paul came and joined the others.

You're a fuckin' hero, lad, said Johnny, I'm requesting a Blue Feter badge for you.

Phil just smiled, embarrassed by it all.

Drinks all round then? volunteered Paul.

We're on large vodkas, stressed Rob.

Fuckin' 'ell, sorry I offered!

The lads walked to the bar interrupted by a few people including the victim.

Thank you, she said to Phil, for doin' that. I had me keys, purse and personal things in me bag, thanks.

Phil smiled and said, No big deal.

Let me get you a drink, I insist.

Ok, said Phil as he walked off with her, winking at the lads and noticing her pert tight arse and firm tits !

More drinks were consumed and the lads danced with partners or alone, performing handstands, back-drops and spins to the delight of the many girls admiring them. The opening bars of "Dancing Master" blasted through the PA which cued an encore. After they finished, Johnny and Rob found a table and sat and talked. The other three continued dancing to the obvious delight of the appreciative females.

I'm taken Barbara out to dinner tomorrow, stated Johnny.

How romantic, ribbed Rob, you must be in love?

Johnny smiled.

Don't forget a single rose, he added, they'll love it and their knickers will come down so easily !

Johnny smiled again.

Chapter Six

It was Saturday evening and Johnny was ready for the dinner date with Barbara. He was dressed as smart as ever, wearing a suit, white shirt and a plain silk tie. A cab had been ordered and he would pick her up at eight o' clock. The mini-cab arrived, Johnny got in and directed the driver to Barbara's. The taxi pulled up outside the house and Johnny instructed the cabbie to sound the horn.

BEEP, BEEP

The sound prompted the opening of the front door and Barbara appeared. The evening was quite warm and she was dressed in a low-cut black mini-dress, her blonde hair swept back and tied into a bun and her make-up applied delicately. She climbed into the taxi helped by Johnny. He couldn't help notice her firm ample bosom enhanced by the low neckline of the dress.
Hi Barbara, said Johnny kissing both her cheeks.
You look gorgeous.
And you've scrubbed up well, laughed Barbara.
Where to? asked the driver.
Giovanni's Ristorante in town, instructed Johnny cockily.
This is for you Barbara, he said, handing her a single red rose.
The stem enclosed in foil.
It's lovely, she said kissing him full on the lips.
During the journey, they chatted, joked and laughed.
Mummy and Daddy are away for the week-end, stated Barbara.
So you've got the house to yourself, confirmed Johnny.
Yeah, she replied with a twinkle in her eye.

They entered the restaurant and waited. The manager greeted them and showed them to their table. Unusual for Johnny, he let her sit down first, guiding the chair behind her.

Quite the gentleman, said Barbara, I could get used to this.

A candle was lit on the table and the menus brought over. They looked through them and discussed what to order. The rose was placed in a tall glass with water, Barbara looking at it regularly.

Giovanni is Italian for John, he said knowingly.

I knew that, she retorted.

Giovanni, Giovanni, he repeated.

I prefer Johnny, especially this one, Barbara said touching his hand while looking deeply and lovingly into his eyes.

Johnny responded with a long kiss.

Come on Barbara, let's order, he said slightly embarrassed.

They decided on starters and fish for the main course. Two bottles of Prosecco sparkling wine was brought to the table.

Hopin' to get me pissed Johnny? laughed Barbara.

Not hopin' love, he smiled in reply.

They ate their meal, drank the wine, laughed and chatted throughout the evening. Dessert was ordered followed by coffee. A musical quartet started to play and they took to the small dance floor with a few other diners. Johnny held Barbara tightly as they moved to the slow romantic music, kissing each other occasionally and passionately. The evening came to a close, the bill was paid and a taxi was ordered by the restaurant.

Dici minuti, said a waiter holding up both hands showing ten fingers !

Grazie, responded Johnny hoping to impress Barbara.

Is that all the Italian you know? she laughed a little tipsy with the sparkling wine.

Si, bella Barbara, he replied smiling.

The cab dropped them off at Barbara's house and they entered the darkened hallway. She switched on the hall light.

Come on, you randy scouse bastard! declared Barbara eagerly leading Johnny up the staircase to her bedroom while clutching in her hand the single red rose !

Chapter Seven

It was a rainy, damp Monday as Johnny dragged himself into work. A tender for building works had to be completed before the week's end and he was chasing up quotes and prices from suppliers and sub- contractors. Between the phone calls he made and received , he thought of the Saturday night spent with Barbara. She was a good lover and knew how to please him. With only one boy-friend, she must have got her ideas reading romantic novels and soft porn, he thought. Anyway, he hadn't felt this sexually satisfied since losing his virginity at fifteen to a married slut four years older.

The phone rang again and he answered it scribbling down the required figures to complete the tender price. The rain had stopped as he looked through the window at the blue sky punctuated by a number of clouds drifting across it. This Barbara's certainly got a hold on me, he thought.

At the day's end, Johnny left the office and walked into bright sunshine. All the costs were in and the tender would be finalized tomorrow and submitted early. He was optimistic that the bid would be successful which meant a bonus.

His home was a mile and a half away and he decided to walk, enjoying the fine weather. The route took him past a small industrial estate, some shops and a church and grave-yard. During the walk home, he reflected on the events that had happened, good and bad.

During the following weeks, he saw Barbara regularly. Sometimes, four times a week and definitely for sex at her house, his house, in the park, in the countryside and even, on one occasion, on one of his firm's building sites in a Portakabin which he broke into. On one date, Barbara told him she would be away for a week in London on a sales course at head office.

I'll miss you, said Johnny.

Me too, she replied in a sombre tone.

She talked about the course in detail which would mean promotion and more money.

Go for it, love, a week will soon pass, encouraged Johnny which made her less subdued.

Chapter Eight

It was a Wednesday evening, Barbara was away in London and Johnny was feeling down. There wasn't a decent program on TV, the football season had ended and he was bored. It was about seven o'clock on that early summer's evening and the setting sun had painted the western horizon crimson.

Fuck this, he thought, I'm off into town for a couple of drinks. One of the cronies is sure to be around.

Unshaven, he changed his top for a white T- shirt and put on a Levi denim jacket which Paul had sold to him a few weeks earlier. The mean bastard had charged him three quid for it !

He checked himself in the mirror, combed his hair and disappeared for the bus.

In the town, he made his way to the Weavers Arms.

JOHNNY, shouted a voice from across the street. It was Paul.

Alright, lad, acknowledged Johnny as he walked towards him.

That jacket looks better on you than me, laughed Paul.

Did you ever pay me for it? he joked.

Don't fuckin' start, grinned Johnny.

I've got a couple tickets for the Oasis, expanded Paul, some student do if your interested?

Too right, lad, answered Johnny, how much?

Don't worry, replied Paul, got them as a favour.

Didn't think you would have forked out money, lad, said Johnny.

Paul laughed.

I'm not tight, just careful.

You're fuckin' tight, stated Johnny smiling.

Come on then, said Paul as they both strode eagerly to the club.

Johnny had known Paul since he moved to Cockshaw ten years ago, both attending the same junior school with Alan. They played football, rode their bikes and generally hung about together. They built dens and formed gangs, allowing only those who bit a worm in half and trapped a fly in their foreskins as members. Obviously, no camel jockeys joined the gang ! At the age of eleven, they went to different schools, Paul to the grammar and Alan and Johnny to the catholic high school. They still hung around, more so into their teens. On leaving school, Paul found work as a house painter which he still did and Alan a mechanical apprenticeship until drugs fucked it up !

At the entrance, they nodded to the door- men who knew them well, produced the tickets and went in. There were a lot of faces they didn't recognize. This was a student do, organized by students, for students. The regular Oasis crowd weren't interested – it being a Wednesday and the tickets in excess of the usual entrance cost. A rock band played loudly on the stage and the dance floor heaved to the noisy beat.

Let's get a beer, suggested Johnny, and we can pipe the new talent available.

But you're goin' steady, Johnny, reminded Paul.

When the cat's away, winked Johnny.

Don't you ever learn? said Paul critically.

You've got a decent girl and you're doin' the dirty on her.

Smiling he replied, Not yet.

Paul looked at Johnny sternly.

You're right Paul, admitted Johnny, I'm a right nob-head but my mate between my legs needs regular exercise.

Beers were ordered and a table found. It wasn't long before the usual mayhem ensued. Drunken students falling over and spewing up, girls in various stages of undress, tables being overturned and glasses flying west. The bouncers were busy ejecting some of these nob-heads as Johnny and Paul enjoyed the spectacle especially the female student nudity and it was only eight-twenty !

Fuckin' light-weights, exclaimed Johnny, I'm glad you didn't pay for those tickets, Paul.

Paul laughed and said

Us lads should go to their fuckin' Students Union and trash it.

I'll drink to that, replied Johnny.

Cheers !

Johnny looked around the club and across the floor stood that Janet talking with some other people amongst them Alan who was up to his old tricks…dealing !

Didn't think he'd let a chance like this go by, said Paul who spotted him also.

Johnny shouted to Alan who acknowledged him and Janet on spotting Johnny, walked towards him.

Hi, she said, how have you been?

Good, replied Johnny, its been a while.

Too long, said Janet who was wearing a black and white striped mini-dress, black tights and black leather boots. Her hair a little longer cut into a bob which made her look a little like Liz Taylor in Cleopatra !

I'll get off, said Paul, giving Janet a good look and thinking I'd like to fuck this myself.

Remember what I said Johnny, he added firmly.

See you Paul, said Johnny his thoughts elsewhere.

Paul walked across the dance floor and joined Alan surrounded by a dozen dip-sticks.

I hear you're goin' steady Johnny, said Janet.

Sort of, he replied.

Sort of....you're always with her, she added jealously.

I'm not tonight, obviously, stated Johnny

Good, said Janet as she kissed him on the lips.

Johnny didn't respond.

Let's have a drink, he suggested, Brandy and Babycham is it?

Yeah, you remembered, she answered.

He went to the bar and waited his turn. A few nob-head students were fucking about but he couldn't be arsed to say something or give them a punch. He returned with the two drinks.

Here's to us, said Janet raising her glass.

Us? Johnny responded.

Yeah, listen, she said, I know you want to fuck me. Don't deny it. In Blackpool you'd have fucked me on me period or not if I'd let you.

But I'm not like that now, he protested.

Are you sure? she queried grabbing his balls under the table.

He smiled and took a gulp of beer. She was right. He did want to fuck Janet. Another notch on his belt but there was Barbara to consider. She'd be home on Friday and normal service would be resumed. He looked at Janet. She was very attractive with black hair, deep brown eyes and an olive complexion, looking sexy in those leather boots.

Fuck it...this is my very last time he convinced himself.

Unusually, Janet bought the next drinks and they chatted and danced awkwardly to the loud noise coming from the rock group. It was nearly eleven o'clock when they decided to leave. Johnny couldn't see Alan or Paul as he walked off with Janet. Stepping outside into the warm night, he asked her where she lived.

Not far by the park, she replied gripping his arm tightly.

As it was about half-a-mile away, they decided to walk. Johnny knew the area, full of smart Victorian houses of which many had been recently refurbished. They strolled past Market Square and onto the park boundary where they stopped and kissed long and hard. Janet allowing him to undo her bra and caress her breasts.

Come on, he said leading her to a derelict house being renovated. They entered through the make-shift security fence and into the darkened house. They were able to see some cement bags on the floor on which they sat. They kissed more passionately, removing some of their clothes, Johnny his shoes, jeans and pants; Janet her boots, tights and panties. After some foreplay, they shagged so vigorously that a cement bag burst expelling the cement powder over them. This didn't deter them as they enjoyed each others carnal delights, gasping and moaning at the climax of their sexual endeavours.

That was good, she said, but look at the fuckin' state of me !

Each was covered in cement which gave them a ghostly appearance. They dressed and dusted themselves down before walking into the street.

I'll never forget this shag, smiled Janet, never !

I hope she fuckin' does he thought smiling at her and thinking of Barbara.

He walked her to her home which was a neat red brick Victorian terrace-type house.

Coffee? said Janet.

No, thanks, I'd best get off, he replied reluctantly.

I'll see you love, added Johnny kissing her cheek.

Oh, you definitely will, she replied opening the door and brushing off more cement from her smart dress while looking hard at Johnny who just smiled.

Alan and Paul were still at the Oasis Club which wouldn't close until one in the morning.

These soft cunts like their pot. I've made a good few quid tonight, stated Alan counting out the cash.

I'd make better use of their grants, said Paul.

Booze and women ! replied Alan.

They walked to the sparsely occupied bar with a few patrons slumped over tables pissed. Two beers were ordered and they stood at the bar drinking. A couple of bouncers came over and woke up the dozing and pissed nob – heads, directing them to the exit.

You know Johnny pulled tonight, uttered Paul, that Janet.

But I thought he was seein' that Barbara.

He is but she's away, replied Paul.

She is a lovely shag that Janet and such a dirty bitch I must admit , boasted Alan, and I'm sure he knows what's best.

Best for him, laughed Paul.

They drank up and made their way out of the club.

On their way, Alan slipped a bouncer some notes of money.

Outside Paul pulled Alan to one side.

Listen, mate, when are you goin' to stop all this dealin'?

We've known each other since we were little lads and you're a good mate but one day this will back-fire on you.

Don't worry lad, said Alan playfully slapping Paul's face.

I'm makin' a good few quid but soon I'll stop. Promise !

Chapter Nine

Barbara arrived back home on Friday. She rang Johnny and they chatted. She was excited speaking to him and relating the time she spent in London.
 I hope you behaved, said Johnny.
 Like a nun, she laughed, and you?
 Oh, yeah. Didn't go out, been as good as gold !
 That was a fuckin' lie thought Johnny.
 I've got you a prezzie, she added.
 You're the only present I want.
 Aahhh, she said, I'll see you tomorrow.
 Ok, Babs, he said replacing the telephone.
 Feelings of guilt overcame Johnny. I've really fucked things up if she finds out about that slag Janet. Too many people know about me and they might gob off to her. Christ, I've got to keep her sweet, he thought. Do I tell her of my indiscretion?
 In the mean time, he got ready for the usual Friday night excursion to the Oasis !
 It was Saturday night and he had been invited to dinner at Barbara's house in Bullstock. He had met her family before briefly when he collected her on one occasion. Her sister, Debbie, who was at university wouldn't be home. Johnny rang the door-bell and it was opened by Barbara, kissing him long and hard.
 I've missed you so much, she said showing him into the lounge.
 Hello, John, said her mother, Elsie, a middle-aged women who had been attractive in her younger days with blonde hair now greying with age.
 Beer? asked Jack, her father without saying hello, how are you or kiss my arse !

Yeah, snapped Johnny in reply, make sure its cold !
How are you and the family? asked Elsie.
We're all fine, he replied.
The small talk continued for a while until Barbara interrupted.
I'll get your present, she said excitedly.
It's from Carnaby Street, she added handing him the gift-wrapped parcel.
Johnny opened it and inside a pair of Logger trousers in dark grey.
They're from John Stephens' shop, she said, I hope they fit.
We'll see, said Johnny as he walked into the kitchen and tried them on.
They fit well, said Johnny re-appearing from the kitchen, thank you so much.
Your welcome, replied Barbara kissing Johnny full on.
Jack coughed loudly, prompting Elsie to usher them to the dining table.
Dinner was served which consisted of steak, potatoes and vegetables. Red wine was poured into each glass.
Help yourself to gravy, indicated Elsie.
The talk around the table was incessant and Jack and Elsie loosened up after a few vinos; his hostility tempered.
Dessert was lemon ice cream topped with honey. After dinner, coffee was served and they adjourned to the lounge.
You've been seeing our Babs for a while now, John, said Jack.
Yes, Johnny answered, a few months now.
I hope your intentions are honourable.
Of course, replied Johnny, I love your daughter.
Barbara was surprised at this statement. Johnny had never told her he loved her all the time they were together.
Good, said Jack, she's precious to me.

Johnny felt intimidated. Her father was six feet tall and muscular, with dark hair, probably dyed. He been an amateur boxer in his youth, Barbara had told him once.

Fuckin' 'ell, thought Johnny, I don't want this cunt on my case.

We're off to play bridge at the Jacksons', announced Elsie, see you later. John can sleep in Debbie's bedroom, if he stays.

Ok Mum, Barbara said, enjoy yourselves.

We will, replied Elsie walking out the front door and into a car.

And so will we, added Johnny winking at Barbara.

So you love me? inquired Barbara.

Yes I do, he replied kissing her gently.

And I love you.

He thought this is not the time to come clean to Barbara.

Why spoil a lovely shag?

They finished the bottle of wine and opened another.

Early night they agreed, taking the bottle upstairs with them.

Chapter Ten

It was nearly time for the lads' annual holiday. Only two weeks away and they'd be off to Newquay. Arrangements had been made for them to drive down in two cars. Fuck knows how the bags would fit in !

Johnny's relationship with Barbara was as strong as ever. That indiscretion with Janet a fading memory but still he knew it was an albatross hanging around his neck!

He had taken Barbara to the Oasis regularly usually Sunday nights and luckily had not run into that slag Janet !

They had been to the Mecca in Blackpool by coach a few times and stayed overnight sometimes, returning to Cockshaw on the Sunday by train.

Over a couple of days, a few of the lads went out shopping or more like shop - lifting for new holiday clothes. These excursions would take them into Bolton and Manchester. Well you don't shit on your own door-step ! Shirts, trousers and tops were robbed during the spell. On one occasion, Phil was able to walk out of a shoe shop wearing a pair of brand new Adidas trainers, leaving behind his manky old plimsols !

A week to go and everyone was sorted gear wise. They could get the Bermuda-style beach shorts in Newquay.

Well, I'm wearin' shorts and tops, day and night, stated Phil adamantly.

And I won't be standing too close to you, laughed Jamie.

Unfortunately, Barbara would not be joining Johnny in Newquay. Her mother was ill and she had decided to stay home and look after her. Elsie had been over-doing it and the doctor recommended bed rest and had prescribed sleeping pills. Johnny liked Elsie and wished her better. He was disappointed but there would be other holidays with Barbara.

Two cars would leave Cockshaw on the Friday night after the pub had closed and drive down to Cornwall through the night. Johnny had packed his large hold-all with a lot of clothes more than enough for the holiday. He'd been to the bank and withdrew enough cash to last. No guest house had been booked and it was hoped vacancies would be found, otherwise it would be kipping in the car or on the beach.

It was Friday night and his father would drive him into town to the Weavers Arms. He kissed his mother good-bye and got into the car. The short journey was made and Johnny bade his father farewell.

Here son, said his dad putting some money into his hand.

It was ten-thirty when he walked into the pub. Everyone was there. Just enough time for a small beer. The lads were noisy, shouting and joking, psyched up for the holiday. Johnny spotted Alan who waved a plastic bag at him. Idiot he thought, those Cornish cunts won't be lenient if he's caught dealing.

It was time to go and the lads piled into the two cars parked around the corner. Rob wasn't there. Woman trouble. He would be coming down later, if Jane would allow. That meant Johnny, Alan, Paul, Phil and Jamie, would be en-route to the west coast in one car. Others from the town had planned to go that same week. Cockshaw-on-Sea it would become !

The cars, loaded with luggage, drove off, out of town and on to the M6 motorway southbound. Another six hours and they would be in Newquay.

Chapter Eleven

The drive down was uneventful. The roads were quite empty considering it was summer and the west country is always popular. The other car had over-taken them en-route and was sure to be in Newquay somewhere.

It was daybreak when they drove into the resort. The sun had barely risen in the east. Jamie and Paul had shared the driving, in the rented Ford Zephyr, without argument. The early morning salt air had filled their nostrils and the sound of seagulls had greeted their bleary disposition. The car had been parked on Narrowcliffe sea front, a road with large hotels nestling side by side with each other. Below them was an expansive sandy beach and beyond that the white surf of the Atlantic Ocean. The beach was completely deserted except for a few gulls picking at the litter bins around the concrete concourse to the beach entrance.

Come on, said Jamie, I'm off for a swim. It'll wake us up.

Johnny and the others followed suit running down the concrete steps leading to the beach. They discarded their clothes and immersed themselves in the sea. They swam and generally messed about in the refreshing but cold salt water. In the near distance, a sailing boat could be seen heading for the harbour followed by a number seagulls of which two dive-bombed Phil who responded by shouting FUCK OFF.

They're after your little worm, Phil, laughed Jamie.

The sun had now risen above the horizon and its warmth counteracted the shivers from the lads as they walked out of the sea.

We've got no fuckin' towels, Phil moaned.

We'll be dry soon, said Alan reassuringly wrapping his arms about his body; his teeth chattering.

They collected their clothes from the beach and made their way back to the car. It was decided that the lads would find a cafe and then some digs. Having parked the car in Newquay town centre, a cafe was located and they all piled in. They ordered tea and bacon buttys. These were scoffed rapidly and the tea drunk just as fast.

We're after some digs, Alan said to the owner of the cafe, a small plump woman with red hair.

My cousin may have some rooms available, she said.

Here's the address. It's just up the road, she added writing it down.

The Happy Retreat was a large guest house near the town centre with car-parking to the front. It appeared neat and clean.

This'll do agreed the lads.

They went in and were greeted by a stout woman in her fifties similar in looks to the cafe proprietor.

We're after some rooms? said Alan.

I've got two doubles, she answered, and I can put a single bed in one of them to accommodate you.

That should do us, said Alan. The others nodded in agreement !

A price was agreed and the stout lady showed them the rooms.

The rules are on the back of the door which I expect to be followed. You'll each get a key for the room and there'll be no fornicating, she said sternly, and breakfast is at nine sharp !

She left and returned to the reception.

No fornicatin', muttered Phil, does that mean no wankin'?

Oh, it does, said Jamie, so you're fucked !

Fuck off, Phil said above the sound of laughter.

Their bags were retrieved from the car and dumped in the two rooms. On the way out they noticed a small bar near the reception area.

That'll suit me thought Paul if it's an honesty bar !

They made their way along the busy Fore Street towards the Sailors Arms. It was eleven o'clock; opening time. The five lads cockily strode into the empty pub and stood at the bar. The Sailors Arms was a very old pub probably built a couple of centuries earlier. It had oak beams and the large bar area was a recent alteration. There was an outside seating area at the rear overlooking the harbour and smugglers in years gone by would have stashed their contraband in the inn having walked the steep incline from the harbour.

What can I get you boys? asked the pretty bar-maid.

Johnny noticed her ample bosom and big curvy arse. The result of eating a cream tea or two hundred he thought !

Beers, love, was the unanimous reply.

The beers were served and they found a table away from the bar. Cigarettes were passed around; they all smoked except for Johnny. The jokes and banter started; the noise and chatter getting louder.

Here's to the holiday, said Phil, and the Famous Five raising the plastic clear beaker containing the beer.

FamousFive, interrupted Johnny, more like FuckYouAnywhereYouLike Five.

I'll drink to that! said Jamie.

What's this? shouted Alan to the bar-maid pointing at the plastic drinking vessel.

The manager replaced all the glasses. We get a lot of breakages, replied curvy arse.

And a lot fights too! added Jamie.

Cheers anyway, lads, said Johnny, here's to the holiday !

The beers were drunk, another round ordered and Paul put his hand in his pocket again.

You a reformed character? asked Jamie.

Paul just smiled.

The pub started to fill up with locals and holiday-makers. It was quite packed when the pub door flew open. A gang of lads from Cockshaw appeared shouting loud acknowledgements, some obscene much to the consternation of the pub staff.

On a box of matches that Phil had bought, and passed around, was a picture of a Cornish ship wreck; one of a series. Johnny looked at the match box and then at two grizzled old Cornish fishermen sat in a corner quietly chatting and nursing two empty glasses.

AND THERE'S ANOTHER TWO FUCKIN' CORNISH WRECKS, LADS ! he shouted loudly, pointing at the two inoffensive sea dogs.

All the Cockshaw lads pissed themselves laughing while some patrons said nothing and others shuffled nervously. The pub manager and curvy arse stared at Johnny.

You say something, boy? demanded one of the seamen slightly agitated.

Johnny smiled thinking they're too old to smack and said patronisingly,

Can I buy you old un's some grog?

Two large rums, one of them answered sternly.

It'll be fuckin' bottled cider, you cheeky cunt ! Johnny replied, smiling as he shuffled reluctantly to the bar.

Me and my fuckin' gob, he thought.

It was closing time and every one drank up slowly.

Any chance of a lock-in? someone shouted cheekily.

No chance, replied the manager of the boozer.

Come on now ladies and gents, we'll be open tonight.

A few lads talked outside in groups, spilling onto the street much to the annoyance of pedestrians and motorists alike. Arrangements were made for that night and farewells said. The FuckYouAnywhereYouLike Five walked together around the town checking on the bars, pubs and clubs that would become known to them over the next week or so.

Chapter Twelve

The evening had arrived. It was about seven o'clock and the lads had got back to the guest house after exploring the town that afternoon. Each had bought a pair of shorts in various colours from a surf shop paying over-the-odds which displeased them. Each had scrubbed up dowsing themselves in potent aftershaves eager for the night ahead. All were wearing their recently acquired clobber and admiring themselves in shop windows as they walked through the town. They noticed a 'chippy' with a couple of customers waiting to be served.

Come on you cunts, said Alan, let's get some scoff!

They filed into the fish and chip shop and a thick set Italian - looking man with a black moustache and bald head took their orders. Three had fish and the other two had pies, all with chips!

Where's the mushy peas? demanded Phil.

No call for 'em, answered the fish fryer.

There should be, added Phil, half of fuckin' Cockshaw is here!

The lads scoffed their meal being careful not to get grease on their smart clothes. Each rolled up the wrapping paper into tight balls and kicked them into a hotel forecourt. A watching night porter shook his fist at them and mouthed some inaudible abuse. The lads responded with a V-sign and soft lad Phil mooned.

With a pub in sight, they each contributed money towards the drinks whip held by Paul, of all people, and made their way to the Great Western Hotel. They had passed it earlier that day and it wasn't far from their digs. This was a large hotel with bars open to non-residents. The lads ordered the drinks and looked around the already packed bar. There wasn't any vacant tables so they were content to stand, talk and joke with each other. Their voices becoming louder with every tale and obscenity, fuelled by the beers rapidly drunk and re-ordered. Alan and Johnny wandered outside into the warm evening air. Alan rolled a joint and lit it. At the side of the hotel was a narrow road which led down to the beach. This could be viewed from the wall by the bend in the road. It was as expansive and similar to the beach adjacent. A few people were still on the beach as the western sun descended into the horizon. Something had caught Alan's eye. In twenty feet high letters the word 'UNITED' had been scraped into the hard wet sand, quite visible to Alan and Johnny and most of Newquay.

Look at that Johnny, said Alan annoyed, I'm not fuckin' having that !

Johnny and Alan were die-hard Liverpool reds often going to Anfield and standing on the famous Spion Kop. And Manchester United, their detested rivals, would be subjected to any abuse the pair of them could conjure up !

Come on let's join the others, said Johnny pulling Alan inside the hotel bar.

Inside they met up with the other three. Jamie and Paul were chatting up two girls while Phil was piling change into a one arm bandit.

Alright you two, said Phil kicking the machine in annoyance.

Jamie, Paul were going, said Alan.

Jamie whispered into his girl's ear and she responded by slapping his face and shouting the word MONSTER at him. He rejoined the others with a red weal on his cheek.

What was that about? asked Alan to Jamie.

I only asked her to suck my cock !

A reasonable request, commented Phil which generated spasms of laughter.

The five traipsed out and up the road towards the town centre.
You alright, lad? Johnny asked Alan.
Sound, came the reply but he was thinking of that graffiti written on the beach.
A club was soon found and they spent the rest of the evening drinking, smoking, chatting and piss-taking without incident or Jamie getting his face belted again !

Chapter Thirteen

The following morning the lads were down for breakfast smartly at nine as instructed by Mrs Mardy Arse. They seated themselves amongst the other guests regaling the previous night's ventures. They were wearing the various coloured surf shorts bought and an assortment of tops; each lad had on a pair of flip-flops. Breakfast was quickly scoffed and they headed to the beach, each holding a bag containing their possessions. They reached the Great Western Hotel and walked down the access road with dozens of other holiday makers. The sun was shining brightly and the beach was quickly getting packed. A small cafe was open and a queue starting to form for teas and coffees. The lads had reached the bend in the road and all the beach could be seen. There now appeared to be hundreds of people – adults and children – staking claim to the best parts. The sandy, flat surface would soon be filled with water by the in-coming tide.

Nice one, you fucker! exclaimed Johnny smiling to Alan.

The huge word 'UNITED' scraped into the hard sand yesterday had now the word 'FUCK' written above it in equally sized letters. This would have been noticed by all who visited the beach and half of Newquay. Shortly, the writing would be erased by the in - coming tide especially that obscene word 'UNITED' !

The lads found a suitable place on the beach near some rocks and spread their towels out. They applied sun cream and stretched their bodies out in the hot sun. They didn't utter a word, content to soak up the ultraviolet rays. After an hour or so of sun bathing, Phil was restless.

There's a game of footie just started, he said pointing at a group of lads kicking a plastic ball about.

Let's go and join in.

The others agreed and Johnny said he would stay and look after the gear. The others went, spoke to the other lads and joined in the game. Johnny looked around the packed beach and thought about Barbara and Janet. I've really fucked up if Babs finds out. Will she forgive me? Will she ever trust me? He was really keen on Barbara even though he was twenty. She could be my soul-mate to spend my life with. She's pretty, a good lover, bright and intelligent. All the things a lad wanted.

His thoughts were disturbed by Phil dripping with sweat.

Do you wanna drink? he asked breathlessly retrieving money from his bag.

Tea, please lad, Johnny replied.

Johnny applied more cream to his face and laid back in the scorching sun. Shortly, the others returned as sweaty as Phil and just as breathless.

Did you win? asked Johnny to Alan.

Did we fuck! He replied annoyed.

They were a bunch of Italian waiters from the ristorante and they fuckin' ran rings 'round us.

Johnny laughed.

I'm sure one of 'em was Luigi Riva, the international, chipped in Paul.

No he fuckin' wasn't, nob-head ! said Alan, still annoyed and reaching for a cigarette.

Phil returned with the drinks and the lads sat, talked and smoked. A group of lads known to them from Cockshaw passed by; greetings were exchanged and short conversations ensued. After a while they all went for a swim in the sea, each taking turns to guard their effects.

It was mid afternoon and the lads hadn't eaten except for sandwiches bought from the cafe.

We'll have a good scoff tonight, stated Jamie lighting a cigarette.

There's a steak house in town, suggested Paul applying more cream to his already burned body.

The five laid back on their towels and enjoyed the sun for the remaining few more hours.

Chapter Fourteen

Back at the guest house, the lads were busy poncing themselves up for the night ahead. They decided on the steak house for their meal and strode into town in search of the restaurant.

ABERDEEN ANGUS STEAK HOUSE jumped at them as they approached the front door of the restaurant. This'll do they thought. A waiter showed them to a table and drinks were ordered. Menus were provided and each chose a steak, obviously; four well done while Johnny preferred his rare. The waiter scribbled down their requirements and disappeared into the kitchen. The restaurant was almost full with diners chatting to each other. Shortly the steaks arrived and the lads tucked in. Johnny was still waiting for his steak. Johnny was still waiting as the other lads finished their meal and about to order dessert.

Fuckin' 'ell, lad, said Paul, you must be starvin'?

Fuck this, muttered Johnny who stood up catching a waiter's eye.

OI, NOB – HEAD, he shouted, I ORDERED MY STEAK RARE NOT FUCKIN' EXTINCT !

The other diners looked up; a silence fell upon the restaurant. The lads laughed a little and the manager overhearing this remark came to their table.

I'm sorry Sir, he professed, your steak will be ready soon and any more drinks are on the house.

You forgot my order, said Johnny annoyed.

You fuckin' forgot my fuckin' order, he repeated.

The manager looked sheepish and said nothing.

And we want free drinks all night, added Johnny.

The manager nodded and fucked off not wanting any trouble.

Let's get pissed then lads, Alan said excitedly.
Too fuckin' right, piped up Phil.

They spent the rest of the night drinking the free booze – beers and the spirits displayed in the optics – seated on the stools provided at the small bar. Their chat raucous and loud which unnerved the remaining diners.

It was nearly midnight when the manager ushered them out into the dark, cool night. As they staggered back to their digs, four girls were spotted across the road walking in the same direction. They were noisy and as inebriated as the lads.

Hello girls, shouted Alan.

We're going skinny-dipping, slurred one of the group.

The others giggled as they stumbled along the pavement.

We'll show you to the beach offered Jamie.

Again the girls giggled.

Where are you girls from? asked Johnny supporting two of them by linking arms.

London, said the tall blonde of the group more sober than the others and obviously the leader.

Oh, Cockneys? added Johnny patronizingly.

Certainly not, she replied tartly, we live in Kensington.

Johnny knew that part of London was up-market and these posh sorts were being accompanied by five Lancashire scallies !

And you? inquired the tall blonde to Alan.

We're from the north, Lancashire, he said proudly.

Oh, rough trade, sniggered one of the group with dark hair, a chubby figure and a face like a horse.

Her companions giggled.

The lads escorted the posh girls down to the beach along the pitch black access road; each linking arms to steady themselves as they slowly negotiated the narrow decline.

The full moon slightly illuminated the receding tide as the posh girls thoughtlessly stripped off and discarded their clothes, bras and panties on the beach.

Come on then, teased the tall blonde as she and the others ran into the cold surf squealing as the waves lapped against their naked nubile bodies.

Let's fuck off with their clothes, suggested Phil.

Don't be a cunt, remonstrated Jamie stripping off himself.

The lads quickly undressed and joined them, splashing the cold salt water about at each other. The posh girls giggled and whispered at the sight of the boys nudity. Johnny and the tall blonde were splashing each other, diving into the surf and surfacing. On occasion, he steadied her as she stumbled in the swell of the sea. She was about three inches taller than him but it didn't stop her kissing Johnny. He didn't respond. Barbara's face flashed in his mind.

My name's Fiona, she said, and yours?

John, er Johnny.

Johnny B. Goode, she teased.

Always, he answered.

That's a pity, she winked.

Here was another opportunity for a fuck he thought . Fiona was a plain looking girl with a very slim willowy body and small breasts but a shag's a shag. This posh pussy was on a plate and he couldn't pass on this. They held hands as they walked out of the sea looking back at the others frollicking in the water. Gathering up their clothes, they disappeared behind some rocks quite away from the others.

Chapter Fifteen

Morning came and the lads were hung- over from the night before. It was a result getting free booze but it came at a price. Skinny- dipping with the posh birds was gradually being remembered and the lads were eager to discuss it. They stumbled down to breakfast just after nine and Mrs Mardy Arse wasn't pleased. They slumped into the dining chairs very much worse for wear. Coffee, tea and orange juice was drunk rapidly but the cereals and the fried bacon, eggs and sausage refused.

Who got a shag? Johnny asked the others quite loudly.

We all did it ! came the synchronized reply.

But four into three won't go, argued Johnny.

It fuckin' will, they replied laughing loudly.

Their conversation was overheard by the other guests and a few disapproving glances came their way. Even Mrs Mardy Arse popped her head around the door !

And obviously you did, said Alan looking at Johnny.

Johnny just smiled.

I wonder if we'll see them again, asked Phil, the one with the horse face was a right nympho?

They drunk refills of tea and coffee and made their way out of the guest house and into the bright sunlight.

My fuckin' sore head, Paul complained.

My fuckin' sore dick, moaned Jamie, those posh girls were really up for it.

Everyone laughed as they made their way to the beach. They spent the hot day sun bathing, swimming, playing football, chatting and smoking. Other known lads from their home town came by and time was spent with them but no sign of the posh birds.

It was about six o'clock when the lads decided to leave the beach. They gathered up their belongings and walked up the access road to the street above. Post-cards and pens were bought and they walked the two hundred yards to their digs.

Clubbin' tonight is it then? suggested Alan and the others agreed.

Back in their rooms, they slumped on the beds and began to write on the post-cards which would be posted the following day. Johnny wrote one to his parents, one to his employers and the other to Barbara but he didn't mention fucking Lady Fiona of Kensington !

Chapter Sixteen

That night the lads made a real effort getting ready for the night club. They decided to go out later at nine and in the meantime ponced themselves up wearing some of the clothes acquired on those expeditions to Bolton and Manchester. Johnny wore a pair of faded Levis, a pale blue soft denim shirt and brown Como slip-on shoes. Paul also wore jeans but with a white T-shirt and a Wrangler denim jacket. Phil stuck to his mantra of shorts, surf-style T-shirt and his new Adidas trainers, while Jamie and Alan wore Loggers and short-sleeved gingham check Ben Sherman shirts.

Each reeked of Old Spice and Brut aftershave and soft lad Phil applied some to his bollocks which stung like fuck !

Maybe he thought he would run into horse face. On their way out, they decided to stop at the guest house bar. A young girl no older than eighteen was behind it. She was slim and blonde with a golden tan. Johnny tried to hide any thoughts of shagging this one.

What do you 'ansome boys want to drink? she said in that languid west country drawl.

Beers, please love, was the orchestrated response.

We've only got bottles, she said apologetically.

That'll do, the lads agreed.

She served the bottled beers and introduced herself as Jenny. She said she was a student nurse at the local hospital and the daughter of Mrs Mardy Arse.

I only work here now and then, she explained, but I got me own room.

Jenny giggled as the lads joked about bed baths and thermometers up the rectum. They drank up, bid goodbye and walked out into the warm evening.

That Jenny's a dirty bitch was the general conclusion.

Two burly door-men stood outside the The Rockin' Chuff disco as the lads approached it.

It was nearly ten o' clock as they sauntered inside which was quite dark and punctuated by the throbbing movement of the punters on the dance floor. The DJ sat in a kiosk above the floor spinning discs of loud pulsating music which reverberated around the club. Familiar faces were spotted as the lads located the bar and ordered drinks, (Paul was still the whip master) pausing to survey the many girls present.

I wish horse face was here, said Phil looking quite forlorn.

I know where she'll be, answered Alan confidently.

Where? asked Phil excitedly.

Haydock Park, he replied, she's been entered in the Posh Tart Handicap !

Phil muttered fuck off while the other lads laughed.

Cigarettes were passed around and more beer drunk.

Did you ask her name? said Jamie.

No, replied Phil.

With that big arse and face, I reckon her name is Clarrisa Buttocks, added Jamie which generated more laughter.

The lads split up moving on to the dance floor amongst the many girls dancing in groups. After a while each lad had paired off and disappeared except for Johnny who stood on his own at the bar attracting looks from a few passing females. He watched the antics of those on the dance floor and was reluctant to participate. His thoughts again turned to Barbara and how he missed her. I've been a fuckin' idiot. She doesn't deserve a cunt like me. It's my own fault if she finds out and finishes it. What a fuckin' mess. But Johnny was his own worse enemy; he couldn't say no to sex and there were plenty of women willing exploit his vulnerability. He definitely required therapy, but that type wasn't available in the late sixties !

He drank up and, unable to locate his mates who were otherwise engaged, walked out of the club and onto the digs down the road. He opened the unlocked front door and took out his room key. He passed by the small bar and smiled at Jenny who was cleaning glasses behind the bar.
Johnny unlocked the door to his room he shared with Alan. He took off his clothes and put them carefully away. His money and the room key to one side. He got into one of the two single beds and pulled the sheet over his naked body. The night was still warm and he lay for a while thinking of the obvious. For more than an hour he tried to go to sleep but couldn't; his mind racing with his current predicament. As he lay in bed, he detected the door of the room being opened. Looking towards it, he noticed the shape of a girl standing in the opening. It was Jenny, the bar-maid, who moved closer to his bed. Putting a finger to her mouth, she stripped off her clothes until completely naked and slipped her body into the bed alongside him.

Chapter Seventeen

Johnny awoke in the morning to the screeching of sea gulls outside. It was about eight o'clock, Jenny had gone and there was no sign of Alan or the other bed having been slept in. He's pulled thought Johnny and spent the night shagging elsewhere. He showered and dressed in the required attire for the beach. It was eight -thirty so he left the room and wandered downstairs to the dining room.

You're too early, snapped Mrs Mardy Arse as she re-arranged the cutlery on the tables.

Soon he was joined by Phil and Paul.

Where's the other two? asked Johnny.

Oh, answered Paul, they pulled a couple girls and went back to their caravan in Pentire.

And you two?

We got a knock-back, said Phil, didn't even kop a feel.

Johnny smiled as they sat at their usual table.

Did you pull? asked Phil still upset over the previous night's rejection.

No, I had an early night !

The three amigos tucked into their breakfasts and chatted about the holiday, reminiscing over the past few days.

Rob will be down in five days, stated Paul, I rang him last night.

On his own? Johnny inquired.

Looks that way, Paul added.

The lads finished breakfast, left the table and walked outside beginning the usual trek to the beach.

OI, YOU CUNTS ! a voice shouted.

Johnny knew it was Alan without looking around, who was with Jamie, both still dressed in last night's clothes.

Dirty bastards ! proclaimed Johnny.

Highly enjoyable, enthused Jamie, the dirty cunts fucked like rabbits !

And we swapped, boasted Alan.

We're off to scrub and disinfect our dicks and bollocks !

See you down on the beach, Jamie said as he and Alan disappeared into the Happy Retreat.

The five, now reunited, positioned themselves in their usual place on the beach. Again the sun's heat had not diminished. Each lad was quite tanned but that did not deter them from applying sun cream to their bodies. It was just after noon and they decided to leave the beach and wander up to the town. They gathered their belongings and walked along the long expanse of sand towards the harbour. They walked to the water's edge cooling their feet and noticed that the beach was rammed with people enjoying the beautiful July weather. The harbour was reached and the Sailors Arms remembered. In they traipsed and unusually ordered two lemonades and three Cokes. The manager clocked Johnny from the other day.

No trouble, boys? he said.

Scouse honour ! replied Johnny.

The manager nervously smiled.

They seated themselves outside overlooking the busy harbour with pleasure boats and private craft sailing in and out and a few people fishing from the harbour wall.

Have you shifted your little plastic bag? Johnny asked Alan discreetly.

He smiled.

In the club last night, he replied, cockily pulling out a wad of banknotes.

And the bouncers? inquired Johnny.

Dozy cunts didn't have clue, eh Jamie? stated Alan triumphantly.

Jamie smiled.

Not a fuckin' clue !

Besides the pot, there was other stuff as well, added Alan.

No wonder those birds last night fucked like rabbits, laughed Johnny.

I've saved some for us, said Alan winking at Johnny.

You can fuck off. You know me and drugs, said Johnny firmly.

Alan was as tall as Johnny with brown curly hair often cut very short and had lived with his parents until last year. He was caught with drugs, fined and lost his job as an bricklaying apprentice. This caused an almighty row at home and he was thrown out. He found himself a flat in a shit part of town and continued taking drugs. Through contacts, he bought and sold mostly cannabis with a few pills thrown in. He made enough money to pay the rent and go out and what he didn't have he robbed!

Johnny was always on his case but he didn't pay any attention to him or anyone! He was a mate though and good one if trouble stirred.

The lads sipped their soft drinks, smoked, chatted and joked.

Rob will be down in five days, someone said.

Oh aye, off the leash then, said Alan sarcastically, he's such a nob-head puttin' up with her.

She's got her own business, said Phil, so he's not that much of a nob-head.

They finished their drinks and walked out of the pub into the hot street swarming with holiday makers and locals. They walked around the town buying toiletries, a few gifts and souvenirs which they took back to their digs. It was mid afternoon and they decided to return to the beach for a swim. On the way, they hired body boards from the surf shop, spending the rest of the afternoon and early evening attempting to ride the large waves peculiar to Newquay. That evening the lads were knackered and spent the evening in the small bar at the Happy Retreat. They didn't bother to dress up. Jenny was flirting as usual with the lads and Paul soon helped himself to spirits when she went for a piss. The bar closed and the lads retired to their rooms with Jenny joining Paul, Jamie and Phil for a four-some!

Chapter Eighteen

The days and nights came and went until it was Rob's arrival. He was travelling down by train and the lads went to meet him at the station. The train arrived on time shedding dozens of passengers eagerly walking to the ticket barriers and exit. Rob was spotted walking towards them, a hold-all in his hand and a canvas bag across his shoulder. Greetings were exchanged and hands shook.
Come on, said Alan, let's get a beer!

They made their way to to the Great Western Hotel not far from the station. Beers were ordered as usual and the banter began.
How's Cockshaw? asked Phil.
Much the fuckin' same, replied Rob.
Barbara sends her love, Johnny, he added gulping down his beer.
Alan looked at Johnny who just nodded.
After a few more beers they left the hotel and walked towards The Happy Retreat and went in with Rob. Jenny was on the reception.
Hi boys, she said.
Got a room for our mate, Rob? Alan asked.
I'm sure we can accommodate such an 'andsome man, she said looking at the register.
A single room's available.
That'll do and you'll do, said Rob looking at her breasts and mouthing a kiss in her direction.
Jenny giggled, blushed and looked away.
I can see he's off the fuckin' leash, stated Alan.

Roberto, to give him his full first name, had black hair and dark features, inherited from his Italian mother and he fancied himself as a player. This stopped when he started seeing Jane regularly who kept a vice-like grip on his balls!

Rob laughed, took the key and went to the room, dumping his bags and returning to the others in the bar. It wasn't open yet but they sat around and talked. That evening, the sextet got ready, had a meal not at the steakhouse, went to a few bars and ended up back at the guest house. A few more beers were sunk and they retired without incident.

All the lads were down as usual for breakfast and a place for Rob was made at their table. The weather had cooled due to the cloudy sky but it was still warm and they continued their daily excursion to the beach. They laid down their towels in the usual place and noticed the same people around them. A few good mornings were said and they settled down with newspapers and magazines. After a while, four of them decided to go swimming leaving Rob and Johnny behind.

Everything ok with Jane? asked Johnny.

Fine.

She was ok with you coming here?

Oh yeah, said Rob.

So you'll be getting' engaged then?

I don't know about that, shrugged Rob.

And here's me about to arrange your stag do, laughed Johnny.

The others returned from the swim and Phil went to the cafe and shortly returned with six coffees.

You're a good lad, said Alan appreciating the hot drink after the swim.

Look, said Paul pointing to a group of five figures kicking a ball to each other.

It's those fuckin' Italians, said Phil.

Yeah, added Alan, they beat us when we played them days ago.

Let's have a re-match, suggested Rob himself a useful player who once had a trial with Tranmere Rovers!

Alan and Rob walked over and spoke to the Italians; a re-match was arranged. Phil would stay and guard the belongings while the other five prepared for revenge.

England versus Italy. Small rocks were gathered for goalposts and the five-a-side game commenced.

Come on lads, urged Alan, let's get into these cunts!

The game kicked off with the Italians keeping possession. They shot and Paul, keeping goal, saved. The lads attacked and Johnny who beat one opponent slipped the ball to Alan. He was tackled and dispossessed, allowing the opposition to pass the ball precisely to each other. The lads couldn't get near the ball; they were chasing shadows. Another shot at their goal flew wide. The lads attacked and Rob, dribbled, feinted and shot, just missing the goal. The Italians regained possession but just kept passing the ball around making the lads look like nob-heads.

Fuck this, muttered Rob as he lunged at one of the opposition with the ball, heavily kicking the back of his leg.

CRUNCH!

The Italian was pole-axed and his team-mates surrounded Rob shouting in their native tongue. He understood their abuse and as the lads rushed to his side he shouted

VAFFANCULO, FIGLIO DI PUTTANA.

All hell broke loose and a few fists were thrown. Rob was restrained by Alan and the Italians helped their injured compatriot away, gesticulating as they went. This action triggered the lads to shout further abuse accompanied with obvious hand signals.

That's a fuckin' shame, said Paul, I fancied some spaghetti tonight !

This remark lightened the moment and they rejoined Phil oblivious to everything; his nose buried in a 'Men Only' magazine.

Rob was unscathed as he sat down on the soft sand and lit a cigarette. A few people had noticed the commotion and came over.

Amongst them was Jenny from the guest house who was wearing a pink bikini. She sat down next to Rob who took notice of her shapely tanned figure.

You're not in work today? asked Johnny.

No, does it look like it? she answered sarcastically, her attention diverted to Rob.

Hi Jenny, said Paul, Jamie and Phil.

Hi, boys, she replied with a broad grin on her face.

She turned to Rob and started chatting with him. What a fuckin' slag thought Johnny. He joined the other lads and the assembled few. The talk was of the incident which was storm in a tea-cup. No-one was injured just a bit of testosterone being expelled. Johnny noticed Rob and Jenny talking and laughing. Her hand was on his thigh as she moved closer whispering in his ear. He responded and they both stood up, shaking the towel and picking up his bag. They moved off, walking to the water's edge where they splashed each other playfully with seawater. Johnny watched them as they walked the length of the beach and out of sight. Five minutes away from Jane and he's actin' like Jack-the-Lad thought Johnny. She won't be fuckin' pleased if she finds out. He had his own problems to put in order and, anyway, he and the others had shagged Jenny so Rob was welcome to her.

I'm off for a beer, declared Johnny, anyone comin'?

Me, said Phil throwing his girlie magazine to one of the others.

I don't want those pages sticking together, he instructed.

Fuck off Phil was the response.

The two of them walked to the Great Western Hotel at the top of the cliff, along the access road which they had trod many times. It was about one-thirty when they walked in and ordered, you've guessed, a couple of beers. The bar was pretty empty and they put some money in the Juke Box. Johnny was mad keen on the Beatles, having seen them a couple of times at the Cavern club in Liverpool and on tour in the local cinema when they became famous. He put on a couple of their hits along with Ferry 'Cross the Mersey by Gerry Marsden. They also decided to play some pool and put a coin in the table. The balls cascaded down and Phil spotted them up. Each took a sip of beer and Johnny broke.

How you doin' Phil? asked Johnny
I'm ok.
You sure? he asked again.
Yeah Johnny, yeah.
Listen, said Johnny, we may take the piss but your a mate and a good one.
Thanks.
It's all harmless banter you know, reassured Johnny.

Phil potted several balls in succession.
Fuckin' 'ell Phil ! said Johnny missing a vital pot.
Phil sunk the black. Game over.
That's a fiver you owe me Johnny, crowed Phil.
In you fuckin' dreams !

They found a table and talked, exchanging shagging exploits, laughing and joking and supping beer. More beer was ordered and the banter continued.
ALRIGHT THERE LA', shouted a voice across the bar.
Johnny looked around. It was Billy, another scouser carrying the biggest portable Hi-Fi he had ever seen. He dumped it on the bar and pressed the PLAY button. Music pumped out of the

speakers attracting the attention of the few customers in the bar.

You can't play that in here, protested a barman.

Who fuckin' can't? snarled Billy looking aggressively at him.

I'll get the manager, said the barman shitting himself!

Get who you fuckin' like, nob-head, egged on Billy.

The barman turned away, his face pale, making himself scarce.

Johnny and Billy hugged. They had known each other in Liverpool, as kids, before Johnny moved. They had kept in touch with Billy often staying at his house in Cockshaw. Alan and a couple of the others had met him on a few occasions.

The bar manager appeared and approached Billy who stood up, whispered something in the manager's ear which made him fuck off.

This is Phil, a mate, said Johnny introducing him.

I'll have a beer then Phil, said Billy expectantly.

And in a straight glass, he added.

I don't want one of them fuckin' mugs!

And me, said Johnny as Phil went to the bar.

What are you doin' here? asked Johnny.

Workin' as a chef at the Excelsior Hotel. It's not far from here.

I know it, replied Johnny.

And I'm not short of pussy, know what I mean.

And the Hi-Fi? inquired Johnny.

Liberated it from Radio Rentals, winked Billy.

You robbin' twat! laughed Johnny.

Phil returned with the beers.

Cheers lads! said Billy clinking the glasses and taking a large gulp.

We're on holiday, informed Johnny, there's a few of us.

And are your cocks gettin' exercised?

Regularly, said Phil.

Right, said Billy gulping the rest of the beer down, I've got dinner to cook, see you later. Come over to the hotel and we'll have a beer.

We will, agreed Johnny. Good to see you, lad.

Billy walked to the bar, picked up the Hi-Fi, snarled at the barman and walked out of the hotel; his six feet muscular frame filling the doorway.

What a hard bastard he is, said Johnny to Phil.

I'm glad he's a mate!

They finished their drinks and bought more. They were wondering to play more pool when Johnny spotted posh Fiona with a mate in the bar. It wasn't horse face but a more attractive girl.

Johnny nudged Phil who looked in their direction.

Let's call them over, he said.

Johnny beckoned to Fiona who waved and came over with her companion.

Hello you, she said to Johnny happy to see him.

Hi, I haven't seen you around.

No, she answered, we've been to other beaches and surfing on Fistral Bay.

Surfin'?

Oh, it's such great fun, she enthused, I learned to surf when I was younger.

Skinny- dipping is better fun, laughed Johnny.

Both girls giggled and blushed slightly.

This is Samantha, said Fiona looking at Phil, remember?

Phil smiled. That night was just a blur to him; he could only remember horse-face and her big arse bouncing in the moon-light !

You girls wanna drink? asked Phil courteously.

No, thanks, answered Samantha clutching a half drank orange juice.

No, I'm fine, echoed Fiona.

Both girls were wearing denim shorts and bikini tops. Each carried a straw beach bag and the fine weather had tanned both their bodies.

Listen, said Johnny, the pop group Small Faces are playin' at the theatre tonight if you wanna go?

We'd love to, replied Fiona, yah!

A double date, squealed Sam, sounds yummy.

Ok, said Johnny, I'll get the tickets later.

Arrangements were made for that evening and the girls departed, kissing the lads' cheeks.

It was nearly closing time when Johnny and Phil drank up and proceeded back to the beach. They rejoined the other three who were chatting and smoking.

Where's Rob, asked Alan, I thought he was with you two?

No, he fucked off with that Jenny.

There'll be trouble, added Paul.

Guess who we've seen, said Johnny, Billy?

Not nut-case Billy, said Alan, fuckin' 'ell.

He's workin' down here in the Excelsior Hotel.

That's a posh place, said Jamie, he'll rob them blind!

We're meetin' him for a beer tomorrow.

We, said Alan. Leave me out !

He'll be disappointed, said Johnny, and he won't take kindly if you blank him.

Alright, said Alan reluctantly, but I'm not lendin' him any fuckin' money. I never got back the last lot!

Club or pub tonight? said Jamie.

Well me and Johnny have a date, interrupted Phil.

Who with? asked Paul doubting Phil.

Two of those posh birds from the other night.

You fuckin' lucky bastards, said Paul enviously.

Chapter Nineteen

The evening came and the lads were getting ready to go out and there was no sign of Rob.
 He's shaggin' somewhere, suggested Jamie.
 In his room, I bet, said Alan.
 Let's go and knock for him, Phil said, catch him fuckin' out.

Johnny, Alan and Phil made their way to Rob's room. They listened and tried the locked door. Alan knocked loudly. No reply. He knocked again. The door opened and Rob stood before them, a towel covering his privates!
 What do you fuckin' want? he said in a belligerent manner.
 Beyond him in his bed was Jenny and another girl, younger than her, both naked.
 She waved at the lads while the younger girl hid her nudity with a bed sheet.
 I don't suppose you're comin' out? said Johnny.
 No, I've got my hands and cock full !
 He closed the door and the lads walked down to reception where
 Mrs Mardy Arse stood.
 Have you boys seen my Jenny? she said politely.
 She and her sister were supposed to be helping me around the guest house.
 No came the reply and they walked on to the front door.
 They're helpin' Rob get a hard on, sniggered Phil.
 Rob's playin' Happy Families, said Alan.
 He'll be shaggin' the mother next.
 What a thought, grimaced Jamie.
 I wouldn't even shag her with Phil's.
 I would, said Phil unashamed.

You'd shag a trapped rat! added Johnny.
Everyone laughed even Phil.

Outside they went their separate ways; Johnny and Phil to meet the debutantes and the other three into town.

Outside the theatre a crowd had gathered to go in. Fiona and Sam were waiting away from the crowd and Johnny spotted them. Both were wearing expensive looking mini-dresses and flat shoes; each carrying a clutch bag. Sam was as tall as Phil with short dark hair cut like Twiggy the model. The lads greeted their dates, kissed them on the cheeks and queued up with the many others. The Small Faces had been popular in the early and mid - sixties influencing the Mod look; a style copied by a generation including all the lads who wore smart fashionable clothing popular on the continent, particularly in Italy. Johnny and Phil had made an effort for the date, both wearing smart slacks, Ben Sherman button-down collared shirts, light-weight single breasted jackets and applying liberal amounts of after-shave.

You look gorgeous, girls, said Johnny.

I should think so, replied Fiona, they're Mary Quant originals referring to the mini-dresses.

Did she say Mary Cunt? asked Phil quietly.

No, nob-head!

Come on, said Johnny as they entered the theatre and found their seats, each holding their respective dates hands.

It wasn't long before the group came on stage, belting out the opening number – All Or Nothing to rapturous applause. Further songs, including Tin Soldier, Itchycoo Park and Sha-La-Lee, got the audience going and the quartet themselves clapping along to the beat. The girls were quite excited with the concert, clapping and cheering each number. The concert ended to tumultuous applause.

They left the theatre, the girls were still buzzing with the occasion.

It's only a concert, said Phil.

But we've never been to one before, admitted Fiona animated.

Let's have a drink, recommended Phil.

Rather, said Sam quite excited by the prospect.

But where? asked Fiona anxious to consume alcohol.

Back at our digs, said Johnny, about a ten minute walk away.

And we can sleep there as well? she asked with a look of anticipation.

Maybe, replied Johnny.

The girls linked arms with the lads as they walked through Newquay avoiding the drunks and nob-heads spewing out of the bars and clubs. They reached the guest house and entered the small bar which was empty except for a couple quietly talking. An elderly man who they had never seen before was behind the bar.

We'll each have a white wine spritzer, said Fiona looking at herself in a compact case and applying pink lipstick.

Johnny ordered the drinks which included the usual beers. Phil and Samantha snuggled closer busy chatting and kissing occasionally.

Cheers, said Johnny clinking his glass with Fiona.

Salute, she replied sipping the spritzer slowly.

So when are you leavin'? Johnny inquired.

On Friday, the day after tomorrow, she replied, back to Kensington and then in a few weeks, school.

School!

Oh, yah a private school in Berkshire, she stated.

So how old are you?

I thought I told you, Fiona said finishing the spritzer and unconcerned with the question.

No.

Well, I'm sixteen the same age as Sam and the others!

I thought you were older, said Johnny.

No! To be honest, you're only my second sexual encounter and I want you again that's why I'm here. My first time was very disappointing!

Fuckin' 'ell thought Johnny, almost a virgin and almost under-age! That would definitely fuck things right up with Barbara. Me fuckin' a school-girl.

Johnny looked at Phil and caught his eye. He nodded indicating towards the toilet.

Johnny excused himself saying he wanted a piss; Phil followed.

In the Gents, they discussed the girls.

They're school-girls, said Johnny, only sixteen!

Phil didn't seem perturbed.

That Sam is really up for a fuck, he said unconcerned.

And so is Fiona, said Johnny, but I don't wanna get involved with a young teen again. I'm in enough trouble as it is with that Janet business!

But it's only a holiday fuck, reassured Phil, we'll never see them again and it won't get back to Cockshaw.

I'm not too sure, replied Johnny unconvinced.

Let's get them a taxi and make some excuse.

The lads rejoined the girls who had ordered more drinks.

Listen girls, said Johnny, I've just realized we need to be up early so we'll order you a taxi.

Oh, that's a disappointment, said Fiona.

Yah, echoed Sam, but we'll see you tomorrow gulping down the second spritzer.

Yeah, said Phil, I'll look out for you.

And will you look out for me too, said Fiona to Johnny finishing her drink with haste.

Oh, yeah, count on it, lied Johnny who went to the bar and asked the barman to order a cab.

The taxi shortly arrived, goodbyes were said and they drove away.

Phil and Johnny had another beer reflecting on the night.

Not like you to turn down a shag, said Phil himself disappointed that his cock wouldn't be employed!

Maybe I've grown up!

Chapter Twenty

Johnny was up early the following morning. He walked along the sea front breathing in the salt air and looking at the deserted beach below. In a shop, he bought a newspaper and chewing gum. Making sure he had plenty of coins, he located a phone box and dialled.

Hello.

He recognized the voice, it was Barbara.

Hi, love, he said.

Johnny, I'm missing you so much. When will you be home?

Saturday.

Good.

How's your Mum?

A lot better, thanks. How's the holiday.

Good.

I hope you're behaving yourself, she teased.

Oh, yeah.

I bet!

Swimmin', sun-bathin' and sleepin'.

No drinking? she asked.

Only occasionally.

Barbara laughed.

See you soon, Johnny. I'll be counting the days. Love you.

And you. Take care.

Johnny replaced the receiver and thumped the coin box. No joy!

By talking to Barbara he felt less guilty about cheating on her. But he had, three times and the most dangerous one was slag Janet who lived in their town!

He strolled back to the guest house and returned to the room he shared with Alan who was still asleep, his clothes strewn all over. Johnny brushed his teeth in the en-suite, went downstairs taking the newspaper with him. He sat in the dining room, much to the angst of Mrs Mardy Arse, reading the news. Liverpool had signed a new player, which pleased him but the Beatles were splitting up, which displeased him. It wasn't long before he was joined by the others including Rob.

Alright lads, said Johnny, all had a good night?

Yeah, yeah came the reply.

And you certainly did, Johnny added, looking at Rob who smiled and answered.

Never had sisters before and the younger one was only sixteen and a virgin !

If Mardy Arse complains about blood on the sheet, I'll say I had a nose bleed, laughed Rob.

Those two we were with last night were only sixteen, said Johnny.

We'll be known for cradle snatchin' back in Cockshaw, boasted Phil.

We fuckin' won't, said Johnny, you'll keep your gob shut!

Paul, Jamie and Alan looked at them.

You mean those posh birds were sixteen?

Yeah, all classmates at a private school.

Fuckin' 'ell, said Alan, barely legal!

We sent them off in a taxi, said Phil.

Pity, the pair of them were beggin' for it.

That's not surprisin', Jamie said.

We were at it 'til nearly dawn with three of 'em on the beach.

Four ! added Johnny.

Breakfast was served which the lads scoffed and gulped down cups of coffee and tea. Just two more days left and then back to Cockshaw.

It was nine-forty when the lads finished and left the dining room.

Let's go and see Billy, said Johnny, and find out about tonight.

Do we have to, replied Alan, he's a mad twat; there's bound to be trouble when he's around.

Hey, said Johnny, if there is we can handle it. Billy's a mate.

Your mate!

The six of them walked along Narrowcliffe until they reached the Excelsior Hotel, past the front entrance and down a side alleyway. The kitchen door was visible and Johnny knocked on it. The door was opened by a Kitchen Porter.

Is Billy there?

Billy heard Johnny and came to the door.

Alright, lads, he said, walking out of the kitchen.

I'M HAVIN' A BREAK, he shouted back at the kitchen staff.

He wasn't bull-shitting about being a chef, dressed in whites and wearing a chefs' cap on his head.

About tonight? Johnny said.

Ok, said Billy lighting a cigarette, I'll meet you in the Great Western at nine and then after we'll come back here. We'll be sound in the bar.

Sound, said Johnny.

Staring at Alan, Billy said,

Lends a few quid?

You can fuck off, he replied nervously.

Billy looked at him, then laughed.

Alan laughed too.

I'll have to go, said Billy throwing away the cigarette, see you later.

Come on you lazy cunts, he shouted at the staff as he walked back into the kitchen. We've got lunch to prepare !

The lads walked to the front of the hotel and stood and talked.

Is it the beach? said Jamie.

No-one answered.

There's a zoo here, Paul said.

Can you imagine soft lad at the zoo, said Alan indicating to Phil.

Last year was enough in Spain and that fuckin' bull.

I was pissed, said Phil defensively.

You and animals don't mix, said Alan.

Not unless he's shaggin' some dog from Cockshaw, added Paul.

Everyone laughed.

Let's just walk around town, said Paul.

The lads agreed and proceeded down the road, past the Great Western Hotel, the Hasty Tasty cafe, post office and police station.

Has anyone seen any coppers while we've been here? asked Jamie.

Each lad shook their head.

I hope no police are about tonight, said Alan, especially with Billy in tow.

They walked further into town to the busy main street, walking into several shops without buying anything.

I need to get some prezzies! said Paul.

There'll be time tomorrow, reassured Rob.

I need some stuff too, added Johnny.

Down an alley off the main street was a man's boutique, L'Uomo, selling mens' high fashion Italian clobber at high fashion prices. All the lads walked in which unnerved the young shop assistant, a lad in his teens.

Good morning, gentlemen, looking for anything in particular.

No, answered Alan as they sorted through the racks of clothes for sale.

I'll try these on, said Johnny taking two pairs of expensive slacks to the one changing room in the shop. The shop assistant didn't see the items he took; he was busy watching the others.

Johnny closed the door. The slacks were the same size which fitted him. One pair he wrapped around his waist, covering them with his shorts and the other pair he brought out.

NO GOOD! he shouted to the assistant, throwing the slacks at him.

There was mayhem in the shop. Shirts and trousers were spread over the floor. Items were tried on and discarded. Someone had turned the door sign to CLOSED unbeknown to the young lad. Each of the lads had lifted something. The shop door opened and the lads walked out.

Rob was the last to leave.

Looking at the young boy he said menacingly,

You won't be silly now?

as he slammed the shop door shut !

Laughing, they ran down the alley and onto the main street. They walked into a small shop and helped themselves to carrier bags in which the newly acquired items were put. Cockily, they walked to the Sailors Arms, sat in the back and ordered beers. What else!

This has been a great holiday so far, they all agreed. We've all had a shag and added to our wardrobe.

And the bonus of a tan, said Paul.

It hasn't ended yet, said Johnny.

Oh, yeah, said Alan, we're out tonight with psycho Billy!

Don't be a cunt, said Johnny, it'll be sound !

Pasties were ordered to accompany the more beer consumed and they stayed 'til closing. They left the pub at ten minutes past three and walked down to the crowded beach through the harbour. Familiar faces were spotted, acknowledged and time spent talking to them. They bought cold drinks from the other cafe which they drank seated on a rock outcrop.

Billy's such a head-case, said Alan.

Alan, said Johnny, don't keep on. He's reformed, he's got a job, you'll see.

They drank the cold drinks and moved on, leaving the cans at the cafe. Venturing into the sea, they cooled their hot feet by jumping at the waves careful not to get their carrier bags wet. They walked up the access road and past the Great Western Hotel which they would visit later. Finally reaching the guest house, they went up to their rooms.

In the meantime, Paul noticing the small bar to be empty, helped himself to half-a-dozen bottled beers. The six lads entered their respective rooms, threw themselves on the beds and opened a bottled beer kindly liberated earlier by Paul. It was about five o'clock; plenty of time to rest.

The lads now fully rested ordered Chinese take-aways. Money was given to Jenny to collect the meals from the restaurant when ready.

What do I get for goin'? she said cheekily.

My cock ! smiled Jamie.

Well then I'll be as quick as I can, replied the dirty slag as she fucked off to the Happy Palace chinky restaurant.

Jenny soon returned with the pre-ordered Chinese food, distributed the take-aways and led Jamie to her room in the guest house. She'll be having a mouthful of balls smiled Jamie to himself and they won't be prawn!

Chapter Twenty One

The curries were consumed in their rooms with the windows fully opened. After the lads had eaten, the empty cartons were thrown from the windows. As they were going out with Billy, they decided not to dress up! They didn't want their best gear fucked up! Even Phil reverted to wearing shorts and a top. They dressed down wearing old jeans and T-shirts. It was nine o'clock when they left the guest house and walked the couple of hundred yards to the Great Western Hotel, going in the side door.

Waiting at the bar was Billy without his Hi-Fi.

Beers? he said to the lads summoning a barmaid.

Finished for the night, he informed them, and it's me day off tomorrow.

It's our last day tomorrow, said Johnny, but we've had a sound time. It's been like home but with sun – shaggin', drinkin' and robbin'!

Good, said Billy, I'm here 'til the season ends in September. Then who knows maybe London to one of them big hotels. Or back to the building site.

The Headland Hotel is open through the winter, said Paul.

No, said Billy, not for me.

The beers were distributed and cigarettes passed around. A table was found, unusual as the bar was rammed. Maybe Billy had something to do with it. Stories and jokes were exchanged as more beers were bought and the volume of their conversation increased.

Billy looked at the lads.

WE ARE THE MAGNIFICENT SEVEN! he shouted.

He turned to Alan and said softly

How's business?

Ok!

Got anything for me?

No, sorry. Sold it all.

Pity, said Billy doubting Alan's answer.

How's your love life, lad? Johnny said to Billy.

Sound. I'm knockin' off one of the Aussie waitresses. She's back at the hotel doin' her nails. She's fit and shags like a rabbit!

Not like a kangaroo, said Phil trying to be smart.

No, said Billy staring at him, a fuckin' rabbit!

There was a nasty tone in his reply.

A silence fell until Alan suggested a game of pool.

I'll play, said Phil, leaving the table holding his beer.

And us, said Rob and Paul.

Jamie also left the table and located a fruit machine.

Fuckin' 'ell Billy, said Johnny. That was fuckin' out of order!

Sorry I know. It was just a joke, he replied regretfully.

Billy was twenty- two and had been around the block. He was short-tempered and this had got him into violent situations.

Phil was playing the second game of pool when Billy strode to the table and handed him a beer.

No hard feelin's lad!

Cheers, acknowledged a relieved Phil!

More beers were drunk as it approached eleven o'clock, closing time.

It's back to the Excelsior then, said Billy as they left the hotel and walked up the road, singing, shouting, laughing and generally fucking about.

Shush, ordered Billy putting a finger to his mouth as they were about to walk into the hotel through the palatial reception area and into the large bar with leather seats and thick carpeting. There were a few guests still enjoying a late night drink as the barman dressed in a white jacket and black bow tie greeted them.

Good evening, Billy. Good evening, gentlemen.

Billy ordered the drinks but no money changed hands. He must have a tab thought Johnny! The talk and banter continued but this time more sedately. The other drinkers slowly dispersed until the only ones left were the seven lads and the elderly barman.

You can get off, George, said Billy to the barman, I'll lock up.

Ok, replied George giving him a bunch of keys.

More drinks, eh lads, said Billy walking behind the bar and filling several glasses with whiskey and rum from the optics. The spirits were brought to the table and those who smoked, lit up.

Cheers! everyone recited.

As we walked past the beach across the road, Jamie recalled, I saw a group lightin' fires.

They'll be havin' a party, Billy said, it happens at least once a week.

Don't the coppers move 'em on? asked Paul.

Not interested and they're not about anyway. Which gives me an idea, replied Billy.

He walked through to the cellar store down some steps in the back where the alcohol was stored and unlocked the external service door at street level. Returning to the bar, he instructed the lads to drink up. The glasses were washed, dried and replaced on the shelves. He locked the cash tills and they walked into the foyer where Billy locked the entrance door to the bar.

After giving the keys to the Night Porter, Billy and the lads walked out and down the side of the hotel to the cellar service door.

It was about twelve – thirty in the morning and the streets were deathly quiet; only the faint sound of the waves and the distant beach party could be heard.

We can't go to a party empty handed, said Billy as he opened the door and walked into the cellar store.

Right, you six carry three crates of beer between you and I'll take care of this, Billy said rolling a five gallon aluminium keg along the floor.

Right lads, let's party!

They carried the booze out onto the street and the door was shut.

I've busted the lock, said Billy, so it's an obvious break-in.

Sorry, no spirits, lads, added Billy.

They've been well locked away!

He started to roll the keg towards the beach and the others followed.

The noise of the keg disturbed the quietness which concerned Billy.

Fuck this! he exclaimed as he hoisted it onto his shoulders.

The road was crossed and they looked down onto the beach which was active with a large number of people dancing and running between several fires. Someone who had a guitar was attempting to sing which went unnoticed. They negotiated the steps down and arrived at the beach illuminated by the burning fires. A few known faces greeted them more interested in the booze than exchanging pleasantries. A place was found near a burning fire fuelled by found driftwood and some beers were taken by the lads. Phil had a bottle opener which he passed around and the bottle caps eagerly wrenched off. The keg was placed upright to settle. Fuck knows how it was to be opened?

They relaxed on the beach, near the fire swigging the beer, smoking and talking. A few girls stopped by and conversations started. Some beers were given to them in the hope of future sexual favours. With the effect of the alcohol, it wasn't long before people stripped off and ran into the cold sea.

Deja vu.

Paul, Jamie and Phil followed suit while the other four stayed minding the booze. More beer was drunk and distributed to a few of the known faces who suddenly became bosom pals. With the lads' generosity only one crate of beer and the keg were left. It was about two in the morning and no sign of the beach party abating. Billy stripped and decided to join the other bathers in the cold sea. Johnny and the other two spotted a group of girls and went over leaving the remaining booze unguarded.

After a while Billy, Paul, Jamie and Phil returned and put on their clothes over their wet bodies. Looking around, Billy noticed the crate had disappeared. He looked about the beach, difficult in the semi-darkness with only the fires to go by. In the distance, he saw the crate and the bottles being removed, opened and drunk by six toe-rags.

That's our fuckin' crate he thought.

The other lads were too busy chatting and flirting with some girls to realize it was missing.

Billy strode over to where the thieves stood. He wasn't happy.

Oi, you cunts you're drinkin' my beer.

Drunk, smirked one of the toe-rags with a strong west country dialect, it's all fuckin' gone. Never mind, you scouse bastard, you can drink your own piss!

This comment was like a red rag to a bull!

You'll be drinkin' fuckin' blood, you piece of carrot - crunchin' shit, shouted Billy, his face raging and the adrenalin pumping.

Gobby squared up to Billy with his arse-wipe accomplices in support.

SMACK!

Billy's large fist smashed into gobby's nose which exploded spurting blood everywhere. The sheep shagger reeled back crying and stumbling about which prompted his fellow toe-rags to attack Billy, kicking and punching him about the body and head. Billy defended himself punching back and kicking out. Blows rained down on Billy from the assailants. The sound of girls' screaming alerted the boys and the six ran to assist him who was now on the floor receiving many kicks to the body. Taking on the Cornish cunts, each lad fought them with head-butts, punches, kicks to the body and bollocks. Billy was free from the assault and able to stand, wading in with heavy punches to any adversary within range. Gobby, who was still on the floor nursing his smashed and bloodied nose, received a few kicks to his body and head!

Rob had picked up a discarded bottle and smashed it across the face of his opponent, gashing his nose and cheek which caused the recipient to scream out in pain.The red blood pumping out like a benevolent fruit machine. Psyched up, Rob stabbed and twisted the jagged glass into the victim's face, causing the tractor boy to scream further like a banshee!

The west country wankers retreated, limping away and off the beach followed by the lads delivering final kicks and punches to their beaten opponents.

They weren't unscathed themselves; each had cuts and bruises and Phil when asked by a girl where he was injured, offered to show her his blackened testicles!

Billy was worse off having been kicked and punched all over; a few cuts were visible on his face and head which were being attended to by a couple of girls.

We all need a drink, stated Alan, but we've got no fuckin' beer.

The keg, Billy said clutching his side in pain and still receiving attention by his admirers !

How the fuck can we open it? queried Johnny.

Smash the top, said Phil knowingly, a small rock in his hand.

He began smashing the rock against the keg seal.

BANG! BANG! BANG!

Again he smashed the rock against the seal.

BANG! BANG! BANG!

Suddenly, the seal was broken and the beer spurted out of the aluminium keg barrel like an oil gusher to cheers and whistles.

This gormless nob-head comes in useful, announced Jamie.

Plastic beakers were rushed over and the escaping beer captured in them. The beakers were filled and passed around and filled again much to the joy of the beach crowd. Those covered in the cascading beer ran into the sea to wash off its stickiness. The flow subsided and the keg was laid on its side to allow more beer to be expelled. The plastic beakers were filled and re-filled and drunk by the lads and everyone remaining on the beach. People were huddled in groups while couples walked off in search of privacy. None of the lads had kopped off ; they were content to enjoy the moment and recall their time in Newquay, drinking the last of the keg.

The keg was now empty and the lads quite pissed but they were still animated and volatile. Groups of people and couples had started to drift away; the fires had died down leaving just the hot embers smouldering. Dawn was breaking and the early sun had not yet risen. Another day was to begin which would be the lads' last in the resort.

Chapter Twenty Two

At the guest house the lads crashed in their rooms, breakfast was missed and they slept on 'til early afternoon. Bleary eyed, the lads washed and dressed and dragged themselves into the bright sunshine. Presents and souvenirs had to be bought and their conversations were about Billy and the fight. They carried their cuts and bruises like a badge of honour. As they walked into town, various faces from the beach party stopped them and engaged in conversation. In the town centre, they visited an assortment of shops selling Cornish wares and artefacts, buying items thought suitable as gifts. There'll be a lot of piskies in Cockshaw !

After they shopped the lads decided to visit the Sailors Arms for a 'livener'.

My mouth tastes like the bottom of a baby's pram, declared Phil.

Piss and biscuits !

They trouped into the busy pub and luckily found a table. Paul and Jamie went to the bar and ordered the beers.

Get me a shandy, shouted Rob.

I knew there would be trouble with Billy, said Alan.

Don't fuckin' whinge, replied Johnny, no-one got badly injured.

Those cunts did, added Rob, smugly referring to the beaten yokels and his handiwork!

The drinks arrived and the lads settled down, quietly talking, smoking and drinking. The pub bell sounded last orders and they declined ordering more drinks. Gathering their purchases, they left the pub for the last time. The lads walked through the town and back to the guest house, stopping on the way at the

Hasty Tasty, a cafe serving fast food, and enjoyed cheese on toast washed down with coffee. Back at the digs, they packed their bags leaving out clothes for that night and the trip home. The hire car was checked over for the return journey having stood dormant for several days. The lads had mixed feelings. They were reluctant to be leaving Newquay but excited they were going back home to loved ones. It had been a roller coaster full of incident ; humorous and serious to be recalled back in Cockshaw.

But their time was nearly over. Just one more night in Newquay.

That night the lads were out on the town for the last time. They found a fish bar called This is the Plaice, and ordered, you've guessed, fish and chips. The fish bar was empty and the lads chatted, recalling their escapades over the last couple of weeks. The meals were brought over and the lads tucked in. Phil even got his mushy peas. It was about seven o'clock when the meal was finished and they left the premises. The lads drifted around the town centre, going into a few bars and pubs but not staying for long.

I wonder how Billy is? said Johnny.

I'll see him before I go.

He'll be alright, replied Alan, he'd fall in a sewer and surface smellin' sweet!

I must admit he's a hard-faced bastard robbin' the fuckin' ale ! added Alan.

They returned to the Happy Retreat and went into the small bar and the clock showed eleven o'clock. Just time for a night cap!

Each lad ordered a spirit and bottled beer and sat down in the empty bar. A new face was serving behind the bar.

Where's Jenny? asked Rob eager for afters.

Workin', said the pretty face behind the bar.

I'm a nurse at the hospital and work with her. She's doin' the night shift this week and I'm helpin' out.

Rob acknowledged the information and continued talking with the lads.

I really fancied a last shag with dirty Jenny, expanded Rob knowing that back home Jane would keep his balls gripped tight.

I reckon this one is up for it, he added looking at pretty face. Nurses are fuckin' sex maniacs!

He walked up to the bar where she was cleaning some glasses and beckoned her, whispering in her ear.

DON'T EVEN FUCKIN' GO THERE ARSE-HOLE! shouted pretty face holding up her left hand which displayed a wedding band.

Rob rejoined the others sheepishly.

ROB GOT A KNOCK BACK! shouted Johnny, sarcastically.

ROB GOT A KNOCK BACK! the others chorused.

Well, you'll just have to be satisfied with Jane's well dipped honey pot! smirked Jamie.

They finished their drinks and left the bar bidding pretty face good-night who smiled and shook her head.

Chapter Twenty Three

They breakfasted, bid farewell to Mrs Mardy Arse, who wanted to charge them for a pissed up bed mattress and loaded the car with hold-alls and bags. They drove off to Cockshaw, managing to squeeze Rob in.

On the way Johnny broke into song -

> #I'm happy I met a Cornish girl,
> Who sampled my clotted cream,
> But sad to leave Newquay town,
> With the rest of my randy team#

This was repeated for several miles; the other lads joining in. After a while the singing stopped and the lads fell about laughing. Silence descended in the car for the rest of the journey and a couple of passengers fell asleep but not Jamie and Paul who shared the driving.

Delays on the M5 and M6 due to road-works, an accident and the inevitable piss breaks slowed their journey but they arrived at Cockshaw in reasonable time and parked in the Market Square. The clock on the tower showing four o'clock. Nothing had changed. It was the same place they left a number of days ago. The grimy facades of the buildings, the lonely people walking aimlessly, the endless omnibuses spewing out soul-less passengers hurrying away. But this was home and a way of life for the lads who had been spoiled by the attractions of Newquay. In a few days, their time away would be just a blur, a memory. No-one had brought a camera so the moments, maybe for the better, had not been recorded.

The car doesn't need to be returned 'til tomorrow, said Jamie, I'll drop each of you at home.

Thanks they said as he drove the motor car on an excursion around the town's suburbs.

Johnny knocked on the door of his house. It was opened by Chris, his mother, who welcomed him home.

Fred, shouted Chris, John's home.

His father came and greeted him.

How was the holiday? he said.

Good, replied Johnny.

You been fightin'? inquired his father noticing the healed cuts to his face.

Fightin' ! echoed Chris.

No, I fell !

Fred looked but he knew the truth!

He followed his parents into the house, dumping his bags in the hall.

Let's have a nice cuppa, said his mother walking into the kitchen and putting on the kettle.

So the holiday was good then? said his father.

Yeah, look at me tan.

His father laughed and joined his wife. Johnny looked around the house. His thoughts of Barbara filled his mind. As well as Janet, the business with Fiona and Jenny should stay in Newquay. I'm in enough fuckin' trouble.

I've got you a prezzie, he said to his mother.

Oh, she said bringing in a tray with three mugs of tea on it.

Johnny fished around in his hold-all until the present was redeemed. He gave the small package to Chris who opened it and asked what it was?

A piskie, he replied, a Cornish elf.

Like a leprechaun?

Yeah, said Johnny.

Oh, thanks. I'll keep it safe, she said re-wrapping it and putting it away in a drawer.

I suppose you're off out later to see Barbara? asked Fred.

Yes, Dad.

You're keen on this one, commented his mother, when are we going to meet her?

All in good time, Johnny smiled.

Chris had cooked a meal and the trio sat and ate it, occasionally chatting about events at home and on the holiday. Johnny was prudent not to mention the booze heist, the shoplifting, the beach scrap and fucking the other girls. After the meal, he took his bags upstairs unpacked them and put his laundry in the basket. He set aside the gifts bought for Elsie and Barbara. Johnny showered and shaved, taking care to ponce himself up. He dressed in the loggers Babs had bought him, a grey cashmere pullover and black Como slip-on shoes with out socks; a cool idea he got from reading an article in Phil's Men Only magazine one day while pleasuring himself. He was ready, taking the bag with the gifts and slipping on his polaroid sun glasses which he, and the others, had worn in Newquay. A mini-cab had been ordered; he jumped into it and gave directions. The cab arrived and he paid the fare, quickly checking himself in the cab window before it drove off. He strode up the drive cockily and rang the bell.

Chapter Twenty Four

Barbara answered the door and threw herself around him, kissing him full on the lips. Johnny hugged her tightly.

I've missed you so much.

And me too, he answered while removing the polaroid sun glasses.

They kissed again, Barbara devouring Johnny's face.

She noticed the small cuts on his face which had almost healed.

What happened, she asked, you been fighting?

No, I fell on some rocks on the beach, honest!

Oh, she said, let me kiss it better.

They went into the house and through to the garden. The smell of burgers cooking filled the warm summer evening air.

We're having a barbecue, she said dressed in shorts and a bikini top, and Daddy invited a few of his friends.

She looked as gorgeous as ever, herself sporting a slight tan. He looked around the large garden and noticed about a dozen people present, talking in a couple of groups. Jack and Elsie greeted him and introduced Johnny as Barbara's boyfriend.

Polite 'Hello's' were muttered.

Beer? offered Jack, producing a bottle which had been immersed in cold water in a tub.

And I'm Debra, said a voice.

It was her sister, dressed the same as Barbara and equally as pretty with the same blonde hair and blue eyes.

Johnny smiled at Debra and was about to kiss her when Babs quickly pulled him to a quiet part of the garden near a timber summerhouse.

Tell me about the holiday, she said eagerly.

Johnny talked intensely and Barbara laughed. He obviously didn't tell her too much. She told him of her promotion at work, Mummy, Daddy and Debra and things she'd been doing. She'd been out a few times with girls from work. The Oasis has been dead without the lads she informed him but she did run into Rob alone. Sly cunt, he thought, on the pull without Jane !

Me and the lads will bring it back to life, said Johnny confidently.

Listen, Babs, he said, fancy getting' a flat together. I've been thinkin' while I was away. I love you, you know that, and even at twenty I want to settle down with you. I've got a good job earning a good wage and with your promotion, we could easily afford to rent a decent flat.

I'd like that, she replied, but it would have to be somewhere nice near Cockshaw Lane.

Oh, sure, assured Johnny, anything for my princess!

I'll tell Mummy and Daddy later. They'll help out.

And you can learn to drive, she added.

Can you drive? he asked.

Yeah, she replied.

You didn't say.

You didn't ask, she laughed. I can borrow Daddy's car anytime.

Well, we can go for a picnic at some remote beauty spot then, he said.

I know what's on your mind, Johnny, she said winking at him.

Elsie called out to say that the food was ready and everyone gathered around the table in the garden on which the cooked burgers, sausage, mushrooms, prawns and bread rolls were laid out accompanied by a large salad bowl. An abundance of chicken pieces and legs were on a separate platter. People dived in pulling at the food in similar fashion to the gannets that Johnny had recently encountered and threw stones at in Newquay!

After the food was consumed, Johnny fetched the plastic bag containing the gifts he had bought. He handed one to Elsie and the other to Barbara. Elsie opened it, revealing a limited edition print of a water-colour of Newquay Harbour.

Oh, it's lovely John, she said, thank you.

She kissed his cheek and Johnny smiled. Jack looked at the gift and muttered.

Barbara opened her gift contained in a small box. It was a silver cross and chain.

It's beautiful Johnny. Put it on me.

He obeyed and fastened it around her neck. She kissed him unashamedly in front of the others who had gathered around.

Jack had brought over a beer for Johnny and a white wine for his daughter. He looked at Johnny and muttered as he walked away.

Here's to us, Barbara said clinking bottle and glass.

Johnny looked around the garden and noticed two burly looking men talking to Jack who had been in his company the whole time.

Who are those two? he said to Barbara pointing at her father's companions.

They're from the local boxing club, she replied.

Daddy helps out with coaching. I think one of them has just turned pro.

They're dedicated thought Johnny both are drinking just soft drinks.

Fuckin' 'ell. This'll be my worst nightmare, Barbara and that Janet meetin' and her old man and these two gorillas on my case and a fuckin' batterin' to follow.

The sun began to diminish, painting a red glow in the sky. It was turning chilly and Johnny was glad of the cashmere pullover. Babs and her sister had put on a cardigan and Jack had switched on the external lights which had illuminated the garden. People were still talking and drinking; a few smoking. The time passed and the guests started to depart. Goodbyes were said until only Johnny and the family remained. The girls cleared up and Jack came over and spoke to Johnny.

She's happy now you're back, he said.

And I'm happy to be back with her, replied Johnny, I love your daughter and wouldn't do anything to hurt her.

Glad to hear that, she's precious to me, stated Jack, his countenance unaltered.

Elsie and Barbara came out of the house without Debra who had gone to bed.

Come on Jack, said Elsie, let's leave these love birds alone.

Goodnight, she added and Jack stared at Johnny.

Goodnight, repeated the love birds.

They sat holding hands and kissing each other passionately. The night was getting cold and Barbara shivered occasionally as the night air wrapped itself around them. Johnny hugged her tighter as they kissed some more.

I won't be long, said Barbara as she walked into the house and retrieved a thick soft blanket. In her absence, Johnny took the opportunity to piss against an azalea shrub!

Come on, she said, walking him to the summerhouse and closing the door behind them in total darkness.

Dawn arrived as they both awoke in the summer house, wearing nothing but big smiles. The sun was just above the horizon as Johnny dressed quickly. Barbara slipped on her shorts and top. They kissed and left the summerhouse with Babs holding the thick blanket.

See you later, love, he said as he opened the side gate.

Bye, Johnny, she replied blowing him a kiss and disappearing into the house.

Chapter Twenty Five

Sunday night came but Johnny didn't go out. He had not arranged to meet Barbara. He was back at work and had to prepare himself. Monday came and he went to work, catching up on the loads of tasks which made him stay quite late.

Tuesday came and he went to work but finished on time. That night he got ready to go out. He was meeting the lads for the first time since the holiday. In the Weavers Arms, all the lads were present except Rob, laughing, joking, drinking and smoking as usual. The time in Newquay and their antics were recalled again and again.

Listen, lads, said Johnny, what happened in Newquay, stays in Newquay.

Sound, sound, came the united reply.

I don't want anyone gobbin' off especially to girls no matter how good it makes you look, he added.

They all agreed again and carried on chatting, drinking and smoking.

Alan took Johnny to one side.

I'm off to Liverpool at the week-end, he said, a big deal is goin' down.

Drugs, Johnny asked, you must be fuckin' mad?

This is mega, said Alan excited, it'll be me last.

Who's goin' with you?

No-one.

No-one, asked Johnny, you fuckin' nob-head?

It'll be sound. I've dealt with the face before.

Where in Liverpool?

Toxteth.

Toxteth! repeated Johnny, it's a fuckin' bad place.

Trust me.

I'll be alright, said Alan cockily.

Do me a favour, take Mickey with you.

Mickey MadArse? queried Alan.

Yeah, answered Johnny.

Mickey was another scouser of mixed-race who had moved to Cockshaw. He was brought up in Toxteth by foster parents and knew the area well. He got his handle from the dare-devil and death-defying scrapes he'd gotten into!

Ok, he agreed.

Here's his number, said Johnny writing it down from the Little Black Book he carried with him which Barbara had never seen or read.

Make sure you ring him, Alan ! stressed Johnny.

The banter continued 'til closing time and the lads departed, catching their various buses home.

It was Wednesday evening and Johnny had a date with Barbara. He met her at eight o'clock at the railway station and they went for a drink in the little bar they often used.

It's a pity no-one took any photos, said Babs, I've never been to Newquay.

I'll take you one day, promised Johnny, you'll love it.

Providing that slag Jenny's not about he thought.

Mummy likes the print. You're in her good books, added Barbara smiling.

Johnny smiled.

Just fuckin' grumpy Jack to win over, he thought.

And I'm wearing the cross and chain. It's beautiful Johnny, she gushed.

And so are you, he said looking into her blue eyes and kissing her full on.

This action caught the attention of the elderly barmaid who herself thought of a similar dalliance a long time ago.

I'm so happy, we're planning a future. I do hope nothing spoils it! sighed Barbara.

They talked until the bar closed and left walking arm in arm, chatting on their way to the empty taxi rank. A cab came along and they jumped into it giving the driver directions.

Mummy's keen on us finding a flat, said Barbara, but Daddy's not so sure.

Surprise, fuckin' surprise thought Johnny.

The taxi arrived at the address in Bullstock.

Johnny kissed Barbara and said,

See you Saturday, I've got tickets for the rugby dance. I'll be around about seven-thirty !

Ok Johnny, she replied waving him good-bye.

The cab continued and he alighted at his house, paid the cabbie and unlocked the door.

Chapter Twenty Six

It was Saturday lunchtime and Alan got ready for the journey to Liverpool for the deal. He washed and dressed, ate a piece of toast and drank some coffee. He had the cash to bank roll the deal. His flat was tidy. His mother coming over regularly to clean and launder. It was located to the west of town in a shabby area. He could walk to the town centre with ease which he often did. He was twenty years old like Johnny but didn't work relying on money made from his drug transactions. He was lucky not to be caught as his reputation was known around town. He was always one step ahead. Today was the big one – cocaine. More expensive than pot but the must - have recreational drug craved by the smack-heads!

He left the flat and locked the door; walked the half-mile or so into town to the rail station. A train would take him to Widnes then a bus to Toxteth. He memorized the address but was nervous, maybe he should have rung Mickey. It was too late. I'm a big man. I can handle this he thought.

The journey would take an hour and half, half hour for the deal and then back home. He should be back for the rugby dance and new customers. The train came and he boarded it, sitting by a window amongst a family. He looked out at the grey sky. There'll be rain he thought. After about an hour the train stopped at Widnes and he disembarked. He showed his ticket and found the bus terminus and stood in the queue for Liverpool. He waited ten minutes and the bus came. He paid the fare and sat on the lower deck. The conductor had agreed to notify him of his stop in Toxteth. The bus steadily motored through the town and out into the country. It passed through the sprawling Speke estate, the Ford motor car plant at Halewood, the airport, the posh Liverpool suburbs and on to Toxteth. The conductor nodded and Alan alighted, looked around and lit a cigarette.

Toxteth was a run-down area of rows of terraced housing, a lot boarded up and those not, leased by slum landlords. He also noticed the giant Anglican cathedral; an imposing structure that dominated the area and skyline. The area was populated mainly by mixed-race and blacks who were descended from sailors of African and Caribbean origin who had visited the port in the nineteenth and twentieth centuries, jumped ship and stayed. Some marrying local girls.

He went into a corner shop and was greeted suspiciously by an elderly white man, standing behind a strong wire grille fixed to the counter and walls, protecting the stock. Alan purchased a pack of cigarettes and chewing gum which were pushed through a small opening in the grille after the cash was received.

Fuckin' 'ell he thought no wonder Johnny and Mickey MadArse left Liverpool!

After receiving his purchases, he asked the shop keeper directions. The elderly man muttered and Alan made his way to Upper Parliament Street. He walked along the street which in its time would have been quite affluent. Large Georgian and Victorian houses, once owned by bankers and ship-owners, had been turned into flats to accommodate the desperate.

He looked at the hardly legible door numbers until he came across his destination. The house was terraced with paint peeling off the heavily barred window frames. It had obviously seen better days!

He banged hard on the heavy door and after a few moments a small panel was slid open and a grizzled bearded black face appeared.

What do you fuckin' want? he growled.

I'm here to see Leroy, tell him it's Alan.

The opening closed. Moments later the door opened and he was taken into the dark interior. A smell that he knew well filled the room and Reggae music blasted from a Hi-Fi somewhere. About half a dozen blacks were present including two half naked white girls.

Hey, my man, said a voice in the shadows.

It was Leroy, the face he had dealt with before but usually on a street corner or in some dingy back-street boozer. Leroy was of mixed-race and a few years older than Alan. He had known him for a couple of years; both had been users before they decided on dealing.

Wanna drink? Leroy asked with two muscular blacks in attendance.

No, let's do business.

Ok, my man, you got the funds?

You got the coke? asked Alan cockily but nervous as fuck.

Colombia's purest, boasted Leroy.

The ship docked only yesterday.

He produced a package which must have weighed three kilos and opened it.

Here try it, said Leroy offering Alan some on a teaspoon.

He rubbed the offering onto his gums with his fingers. He'd had some before and this seemed kosher.

How much do you want? asked Leroy.

I've got five hundred notes, Alan replied.

Ok, a quarter kilo.

FUCKIN' QUARTER? Shouted Alan which alerted the henchmen who moved menacingly towards him.

Yeah, man, you're gettin' pure coke but cut it right with baking powder or crushed aspirin and you can well treble your money, know what I mean?

Ok, agreed Alan, reluctantly.

He was fucked anyway if he argued. The quarter kilo was weighed and packaged up. The money was handed over and Leroy counted it slowly, examining every ten pound note. Alan took the package and put it inside his overcoat which had deep pockets.

Nice to do business, Alan, said Leroy who turned towards one of the white slags who was high on dope and kissed her on the cheek.

Alan said nothing and was shown out of the door by the bearded black man who had let him in earlier.

Outside he breathed a sigh of relief. It was drizzling now as he made his way to Liverpool city centre, about a mile away, where he could get a train directly to Cockshaw. He had spent all his money on this deal but was sure the re-sale of the coke would make him solvent. He walked towards the end of Upper Parliament Street and passed an alleyway.

THUMP!!

Chapter Twenty Seven

Johnny was excited as he got ready for the rugby club dance. He had told his mother and father of his intentions. They both were pleased that at last he'd stopped his gallivanting and found himself a girl. But his mother still expected to be number one in Johnny's eyes.

When are we gonna meet her?

Soon, mam, came the reply, maybe tomorrow.

Hear that Fred, I'll need to clean this place and you'll help.

The house was immaculate but Johnny's mother could always find dirt!

He got a mini-cab to Barbara's at about seven o'clock arriving at seven-twenty. Barbara answered the door as usual, dressed as smart as ever in a new pale blue mini dress which enhanced her tanned legs and matching pale blue shoes. Her long blonde hair shone and she had applied black mascara to her eyes. The image of Brigit Bardot came to mind. He planted a big kiss on her lips and entered the house. He noticed Elsie's gift, framed and hanging in a prominent place in the hallway.

Jack and Elsie greeted him. Jack was resigned that Babs and Johnny would be setting up home and was reassured by Elsie that it would work out. Debra was in agreement, after all she would be getting Barbara's bed room!

I'll be almost your sister-in-law, said Debra winking and licking her lips at Johnny.

A signal that said to him 'Come and fuck me!'

Anyway let's have a drink, said Elsie.

Jack poured out five small glasses of sherry. Tight arse, thought Johnny as they toasted Barbara and John.

They chatted until the cab arrived beeping its horn. It was seven forty-five when the mini-cab drove away.

Where to mate? asked the driver.
Cockshaw Rugby League Club, lad, replied Johnny.

Rugby league was the most popular sport in Cockshaw. There was a football league team but the rugby side got the most attendances and all the schools taught it to its male pupils. The club ran a dance once a month to boost funds and showcase local beat groups of which some had found fame nationally.

All the lads would be there, maybe a couple with dates and, hopefully, Alan safely back from Liverpool.
During the cab journey, Johnny and Babs talked about their plans and were keen to tell the others. The cab arrived and Johnny paid the fare. He and and Barbara made their way to the entrance, produced the tickets and went in, climbing the stairs to the bar lounge.
Johnny was dressed in a beige single breasted suit, a white Giorgio Armani T-shirt and brown Comos; sockless, of course.
They walked into the large bar lounge with a dance floor surrounded by tables. A small stage had a DJ playing the chart hits of the time.
They recognized a few faces who nodded, smiled and waved.
Alright lad, said Rob with Jane on his arm. She was quite pretty with brown hair and a slim figure. Her hair was immaculate cut short in a modern style.
Hi, said Jane, I'm Rob's girl. I've heard about you, Barbara. Make an honest man out of him !
I'll try, she replied holding Johnny's arm tight.
Alright, said Jamie appearing with Phil each holding a drink.
Paul's comin' later he's bringin' a date.

I'll get the drinks offered Rob who took the orders and disappeared to the bar.

I heard you boys had a good time in Newquay, said Jane.

Rob told me what you got up to.

Johnny remembered. Rob wasn't there last Tuesday. He's fuckin' gobbed off.

Yeah, said Jamie, it was eventful.

Eventful, said Jane loudly, nude swimmin', stolen booze and fightin'.

Thank Christ he didn't mention shaggin' thought Johnny.

Barbara looked at Johnny who just shrugged. Rob returned with a tray of drinks, wine for the girls and beers for the lads. They found a table and the six sat and chatted.

Fighting, said Barbara to Johnny, you didn't fall over like you said.

Just a skirmish, replied Johnny, eh, lads?

Yeah, nothin', agreed Jamie and Phil.

What else have you been up to, said Barbara, and don't lie?

Jamie and Phil looked at each other. Johnny's in the doghouse now they thought.

Look Barbara, let's have a good time. It's our first proper date since I got back. Let's not spoil it.

Barbara looked away and took a large gulp of wine. I've been rumbled thought Johnny and thanks to fuckin' Rob.

Come on, said Johnny, let's have a dance.

They went onto the floor and danced to a slow number the DJ was spinning. He held her tight as they moved their bodies to the beat.

Sorry, I lied, he said, I didn't want to worry you. I'm in one piece, it was nothin'.

Stolen booze? she said her eyebrows raised.

Nothin' to do with me, he protested, a mate.

What mate?

Fuckin' 'ell, he thought it's like the Spanish Inquisition.

A lad called Billy, you don't know him.

Your fucking hard work, she said kissing him before they walked back to the table, hand in hand.

And the nude bathing? she asked.

Just lads fuckin' about.

No girls?

No girls, emphasized Johnny.

That's right Babs, said Phil, just us lads.

And where's Alan? Phil added deflecting the questions.

He went to Liverpool today but said he'd be back, said Johnny.

Liverpool, said Phil, what the fuck for?

Business, replied Johnny, business!

Johnny bought the next round of drinks and went for a piss with Rob.

What the fuck did you tell Jane?

Nothin' Johnny, explained Rob, it's what lads do on holiday. Male bravado.

If this fucks things up with me and Barbara, then fuckin' Jenny and her sister will be mentioned.

You wouldn't, said Rob agitated.

Watch me!

Johnny walked out of the toilet and rejoined the others.

You alright? asked Barbara.

Yeah, love!

Rob followed and sat next to Jane who looked at him and Johnny, both staring away.

A local group, Bobby and the Helmets, took to the stage and started playing. This was a cue for more dancing and everyone took to the dance floor. Jamie and Phil had found partners and danced to the beat. After a couple of numbers, they returned to the table.

Sat there was Paul who had just arrived with his date – **Janet!**

Johnny was gob-smacked. His nightmare had fuckin' begun.

Alright, lads, said Paul, this is the beautiful and sexy Janet !

Alright Paul, said Johnny quietly.

Alright Janet, said Jamie and Phil.

While Jane and Barbara muttered a greeting.

You're not speakin' to me then Johnny? said Janet slightly inebriated.

You know this girl? asked Barbara.

He knows me, love, we're very,very good friends! she slurred.

What does she mean Johnny? asked Barbara herself getting quite animated with the conversation.

Nothin', answered Johnny squirming at the question.

She's drunk,love. Don't take any notice.

Paul pulled Janet away from the table and towards the bar.

TAKE HER OUT, shouted Johnny to Paul, SHE'S PISSED!

Fuck off, we've just got here !

Well keep her under control, said Johnny.

Janet broke away from Paul and returned to the table.

You weren't in control when you shagged me, she uttered nastily.

WHAT? shouted Barbara.

Oh, yes, love, said Janet venomously, your precious Romeo screwed me one night while you were miles away. Down in London, was it?

The altercation had alerted a couple of rugby players who came over.

Keep the noise down, lads there are other people, one said.

Sorry, replied Phil, his hands raised in an apologetic fashion!

Paul, embarrassed, came and grabbed Janet who had calmed down, content with the damage she had done.

You went with that fuckin' slag while I was in London, said Barbara her voice trembling, you fuckin' piece of shit Johnny.

How could you? You said you loved me. You told my family you loved me. And you went behind my back and shagged that fuckin' whore!

Her voice was loud and trembling and the others watched in silence.

She was nothin', honey, said Johnny trying to pacify Barbara.

It meant nothing!

DON'T YOU FUCKIN' HONEY ME, she screamed and ripped the cross and chain from her neck, throwing it at him.

FUCKIN' HAVE THIS BACK, YOU CUNT!

The chain landed on the floor behind him. The music had stopped playing and all the club could hear Barbara ranting and raving.

You alright, love? said a voice outside the group.

No, I'm fuckin' not, she replied breaking into tears.

Johnny put his arm around her.

YOU CAN FUCK OFF! she shouted, crying uncontrollably.

Barbara had never sworn like this before and Jane provided comfort by taking her into the Ladies toilets.

Fuckin' 'ell Johnny, said Jamie, you stupid cunt!

Yeah, Johnny. What did you fuckin' expect? added Phil.

He looked at them both with a forlorn and dejected countenance.

Well that's fucked it, good style, said Johnny to them.

Catching sight of Janet, he shouted,

 SATISFIED YOU FUCKIN' SLAG!

Oi, said Paul, watch your fuckin' mouth.

Or, what? responded Johnny squaring up to him.

Several rugby players came over including Jane's brothers and suggested they all leave.

Sorry, lads, Jamie apologized, there'll be no more trouble. We'll look after him. Promise.

Alright but anymore and you're all fuckin' out includin' you Rob said one of the brothers.

And it gets better, said Phil.

I rung Alan's home and spoke to his mother. The police have been in contact. They found his Mum's phone number and ID on him. He's been smacked over the head and robbed. He's in Broadgreen Hospital, Liverpool. It's fuckin' serious. He's in a coma !

Fuckin' 'ell, said Johnny, I need to see Alan. I need to see Barbara. What a fuckin' mess!

Barbara was still in the toilets with Jane as Johnny left the rugby club. He never saw her. Without bidding farewell to Jamie and Phil, he got into a waiting taxi and was in tears as he told the driver his home address.

He arrived home and went into the house.

You're home early, son, said his mother watching some old black and white film again on TV.

Alan's in hospital, he replied near to tears, it's serious. I've gotta see him.

Calm down, said his father.

Chris make him some strong tea.

But what about me film? she protested.

Just make the tea, please, Fred replied.

How's Barbara? she shouted from the kitchen.

Ok, he replied knowing she wasn't.

What hospital is he in?

Johnny gave his father the name and Fred looked up the number and dialled.

Admissions, please, he said as he waited a few moments.

Hello, I'm inquiring about Alan Smith who was admitted earlier. Oh, yes I'm family, his uncle.

He listened intently and then said thank you.

How is he? Johnny asked impatiently.

Alan's in intensive care. He's in a coma but stable. He's got a fractured skull but we can see him briefly. I'll take you tomorrow, John.

Thanks, Dad.

Here's the tea, said his mother, you know I've missed me film.

Fred and Johnny looked at one another.

Chapter Twenty Eight

The following morning, Johnny and his Dad drove to Broadgreen Hospital and parked the car. They went to reception and were directed to Intensive Care. As they approached IT, Johnny recognized Alan's parents.
What happened John? asked his mother, a slim lady with well-worn features, who was crying intermittently.
I don't know Doreen.
You weren't with him?
No, Johnny replied, he was on his own.
Johnny had to lie.
Alan's father, George who was looking through the glass partition at him laying motionless said to Johnny,
Why was in in Liverpool?
I don't know, George, lied Johnny again !

George comforted Doreen who was crying again. Johnny looked at Alan who had tubes and a blood drip attached to his body.
What have the police said? asked Johnny himself near to tears.
Only that he was attacked and robbed. He received a heavy blow to the back of his head. It was lucky he had ID and next of kin phone number on him, related George.
Any one been caught?
No, replied Alan's father, the police are still makin' inquiries.
Anyone want coffee? asked Fred standing by a vending machine.
No, thanks came the answer.

After a while, Johnny and Fred said goodbye to the Smiths. Johnny promising to return the following night after work.

I'll bring you, son, said his father.

Back home, Johnny spent the afternoon thinking about Barbara and what a cunt he was. If my relationship's fucked so is Rob's, the fuckin' gobby cunt. I know that Jane, she loves droppin' lads in the shit.

The following evening, he returned with Fred to the hospital. He was allowed to sit at the bedside. The Smiths had been in earlier but no change in Alan. Johnny stroked his hand speaking to him and recalling their first meeting and all the scrapes they'd been in. For a couple of hours, Johnny talked and talked often repeating himself over and over. His father had gone to a cafe near the hospital and read a newspaper. It was nine o'clock when Fred collected him and they drove home. Johnny repeated this for two more nights and on the third night Alan's eyes flickered. A doctor and nurse came quickly and Johnny was ushered out. Checks were made and the doctor informed him that Alan was regaining consciousness.

More tests are required but we are optimistic, said the doctor who rang the Smiths with the news.

The following night when Johnny and his father returned, Alan was fully awake with his mother and father at his bedside. Doreen was less tearful.

Alright, lad, said Johnny.

Hi, thanks for bein' here Johnny, you're a good lad.

Not in Barbara's books, said Johnny despondently.

How come?

We'll leave you boys to talk, said George as he and Doreen joined Fred for a coffee outside.

She found out I shagged that slag Janet and all hell broke fuckin' loose in the rugby club.

You soft cunt, said Alan.

I am, Johnny agreed.

It looks like our relationship is fuckin' over!

Anyway, what do you remember about your attack?

Before I blacked out, I saw one of the cunts who attacked me. He was with that fuckin' nigger ponce Leroy. The black cunt hit me with a hammer and must have took the gear I'd bought. Today, I gave the cops a description and the address where that cunt Leroy was. But I'm fuckin' broke!

But you're alive, said Johnny.

Just, smiled Alan, trying to disguise the pain etched on his face.

A nurse came in and ushered Johnny out.

Alan needs rest, she said in an officious tone.

He looked at the attractive nurse and was tempted to ask if she had a younger sister but thought otherwise.

See you lad, said Alan.

Not if I see you first!

Johnny didn't visit him anymore. He left that to his family but kept in contact with George. The other lads visited though on a couple of occasions. Anyway, he'd be discharged in a week and back at his parents' house convalescing and he could visit then.

He rang Barbara's house phone and works number a few times without success

That's it he thought, it's all fuckin' over now, to quote the Stones!

Chapter Twenty Nine

Johnny went to work but didn't socialize, still thinking of Barbara and the trouble he had caused. Anyway Alan was poorly, Paul was still shagging that trollop and he wasn't speaking to Rob but thinking of dropping him in the shit which left Jamie and Phil.

For the first time, other than illness, he was disinterested in satisfying the many females available to him in Cockshaw!

One warm evening several days later, Johnny was walking home from work when he realized he was being followed. He thought nothing of it and continued along the route home. He was at the church gate when a voice called out to him.

Hey, you prick we want a word.

Johnny looked around and recognized the two gorillas who had been talking to Jack at the barbecue. They were big and muscular with flattened noses! These were the fuckin' boxers that Barbara had identified. I'm fucked here, he thought, I'll front it out.

What do you cunts want? he said bravely or stupidly.

A word, said one of the silver-backs.

Haven't got time, I'm busy.

You won't be fuckin' busy when we've finished.

Johnny legged it, not down the road but into the churchyard.

Fuckin' 'ell, I'm cornered and my prophesy has come true!

One of them grabbed Johnny who responded by landing a punch. Bad move. A punch was thrown at Johnny landing on his face. Further punches, executed by the two gorillas, rained in as he tried to defend himself. Body blows caught him in the ribs and kidneys and again in the face. He tried in vain to get in a punch but it was impossible against trained pugilists. More rapid punches caught him about the body, face and head. Finally, he slumped to the floor, his face the colour of crimson, swollen, bloodied and bruised. For good measure, he was viciously kicked a few times in the body and arms but Johnny had pulled his legs up protecting his most treasured possession. After a few final kicks to his body and his head being stamped on, the bruisers departed, leaving Johnny bleeding and for dead. He was well battered as he dragged himself slowly to the church door.

Why have thou forsaken me Lord? he pleaded before passing out.

Deja vu.

Chapter Thirty

Johnny awoke in a hospital bed; his mother and father at his side. A passer-by had found him and rung nine-nine-nine. Chris was upset and Fred was comforting her.

The doctor told them he had suffered concussion, a broken arm, cracked ribs, lacerations and severe bruising to the face, head and body but his nose unbroken. Luckily tests confirmed no brain damage but he was under twenty four hours observation. He couldn't talk and could only drink through a straw. Johnny's face was a mess; the bruising had closed his eyes and the cuts to his face required stitching. His left arm was in plaster and his ribs bandaged.

Who could have done this to my baby? Chris cried.

Johnny knew.

His parents remained at their son's bedside until late. For several days, they visited him in Cockshaw Infirmary staying late into the night. He steadily made progress but his injuries still visible.

On one visit, Chris told him that Barbara had rang. She had found out about the beating from Jamie and wanted to see him.

I'd like that, mam, he muttered, please ring her.

Barbara and his mother would eventually meet but not under the circumstance he wanted.

Alan was out of hospital and back home living with his parents. The police had told him that Leroy and his cronies had been arrested and charged with drugs offences and controlling prostitutes. This gave him some satisfaction. He vowed to give up the drugs and even stop smoking. Oh, and find a job!

Fuckin' 'ell he thought I could have been killed!

Things gradually returned to normal. Paul dated that slag Janet a few more times, shagged her silly and dumped her. Rob and Jane were still together, just and Jamie and Phil were the same Jamie and Phil, still fucking about and taking the piss out of each other !

Barbara came to visit Johnny in hospital one afternoon. She was nervous but wanted to see him. He'd been a right bastard to her but she still needed to talk to him. A nurse showed her to his bed. He was still in plaster and his face a mess; a saline drip was attached to the back of his right hand. On seeing Barbara, he managed a smile.
Hi, she said, I'm sorry to see you like this.
It's me who should be sorry. I've been a right prick to you Babs, I never wanted to hurt you, he managed to say.
But you did and embarrassed me in front of your friends, she answered.
I am still upset. You caused me a lot of pain. I knew of your reputation but I thought we had something special and you would put your past behind you. I don't know if I can ever love or trust you again. You don't know this but I took some of Mummy's pills that's how bad I felt. I fucking nearly killed myself over you, Johnny!
She started to cry and Johnny felt helpless not being able to comfort her. She took some tissues from a box on a side table and blew her nose.
Oh Christ, Barbara, he said a tear running down his face.
Please forgive me Barbara, please!
I don't know Johnny, I really don't know.
She cried some more and again blew her nose, discarding the tissue into a bin.
You must feel something to come and see me, he added.
What we had was good but can I ever love you again? That's what I've been asking myself. You betrayed me, Johnny. Can I ever trust you again?

Please Barbara, I've learned a very hard lesson and couldn't bear losing you but I wouldn't blame you if you walked out of my life.

A look of resignation was etched on Johnny's face.

Barbara looked at him without saying anything.

Johnny lifted his right his hand extending it to her but careful of the drip tube in the back. He looked at Barbara who looked at him and smiled, taking hold of his hand with her left.

Alright, but no more fucking lies, she said firmly, no fucking more!

Johnny gripped her hand tightly.

Thank you, thank you, Barbara, cried Johnny tears persistently running down his face.

I love you so much.

She wiped away his tears and stroked his battered face. More relaxed, they talked and talked, Barbara sitting closer, continuing to stroke Johnny's face and helping him sip his drink.

Yes, thought Johnny.

A nurse arrived and took his blood pressure and temperature after which she said,

You have more visitors, John.

Alan, who was assisted by Jamie and Phil, walked to his bedside along with Rob and Paul carrying flowers and grapes which had been half eaten by Phil.

On seeing Barbara close to Johnny, the lads looked at each other, smiled and nodded.

With Barbara reconciled and his mates gathered around, Johnny smiled and said -

Alright, lads!

Printed in Great Britain
by Amazon